The Hardy Boys®
in
The Short Wave Mystery

This Armada book belongs to:

Hardy Boys® Mystery Stories in Armada

* For contractual reasons, Armada has been obliged to publish from No. 57 onwards before publishing No. 53–56. These missing numbers will be published as soon as possible.

The Hardy Boys® Mystery Stories

The Short Wave Mystery

Franklin W. Dixon

Armada

First published in the U.S.A. in 1966 by Grosset and Dunlap, Inc.
First published in the U.K. in 1980 by
William Collins Sons & Co. Ltd, London and Glasgow
This Armada edition first published in 1990

Armada is an imprint of
the Children's Division, part of
Harper Collins Publishers,
8 Grafton Street, London W1X 3LA

Printed and bound in Great Britain by
William Collins Sons & Co. Ltd, Glasgow

CONTENTS

1

The Apeman's Warning

Didahdit . . . dahdahdididit . . . didididahdah . . . dahdidah-dit . . . Frank Hardy's fingers deftly pounded out the CW-key sign-off: "R 73 C U AGN AR WB2EKA DE WB2XEJ SK."

Then the dark-haired, eighteen-year old ham operator jotted an entry into a black logbook. "Coming in clear tonight, Joe!"

"Sure is. Let's see what else we can pick up." Joe Hardy, blond and a year younger, flicked the phone switch and played the transceiver dial along the 2-metre band.

The Hardy brothers, both licensed radio amateurs, were enjoying an hour of short-wave hamming in their newly equipped attic 'shack'. Static and bits of conversation crackled over the speaker. Suddenly a weird garble of nonsensical, voicelike sounds broke in.

"Sufferin' cats! What's all that?" Joe muttered. As a whistling noise began to drown out the gibberish, he 'tendered' the tuning dial left, then right. Again the jumbled voice came in. "Sounds like a tape being played backwards."

Frank frowned. "Must be a scrambler."

"But why would anyone be using a voice scrambler over this frequency?" Joe asked.

A shrill scream from somewhere below caused both boys to leap from their chairs.

"That's Aunt Gertrude!" Frank cried out.

The boy's raced downstairs. In the dining room they found Miss Hardy, their tall, bespectacled maiden aunt, standing with a horrified look on her sharp-featured but kindly face.

"Aunty! What's wrong?" Joe exclaimed.

"There's an ape out there – peering in at us!" She pointed a trembling forefinger. "Great heavens! It must have escaped from a zoo!"

"An ape?" Frank echoed incredulously. The boys turned towards the side windows, straining their eyes to see into the gathering autumn dusk.

"In the evergreens." Aunt Gertrude's voice quivered.

Joe gasped in astonishment. Among the branches he could make out a hideous dark face. Its beady orange eyes glared back at him, reflecting the glow of light from the room.

"Good night! She's not kidding!" Frank made a dash for the kitchen. "Come on, Joe!"

Rocketing out of the back door, the two boys sprinted across the yard and around the house. Frank reached the cluster of evergreens first – then froze, wide-eyed. "For Pete's sake," he whispered, "it's a baby gorilla!"

The animal, perched among the branches, appeared not to notice them.

"What do we do now?" Joe gulped. "From what I've heard, those things are *trong* – even in the junior size!"

"If it did escape from a zoo, it's probably tame,' Frank said.

Nevertheless, the boys moved closer cautiously. The gorilla made no movement. Joe, whose high spirits often landed him in dangerous situations, could not resist reaching out and giving one of the evergreen branches a tug. The gorilla slipped downward slightly, but still did not seem to move a muscle!

"Wait a second!" Frank exclaimed. "That thing looks phony to me – I'll bet it's not even alive!"

He gave the evergreen a harder shake and the gorilla tumbled from the branches!

Joe stared down foolishly at the chunky black figure at their feet, its sightless glass eyes still wide open. "Well, I'll be a monkey's uncle! It's just a stuffed specimen!"

Frank nodded. "But where did it come from?"

"Search me." Joe picked up the small gorilla with a chuckle. "Let's go see what Aunt Gertrude thinks of Junior."

Grinning, Frank accompanied his brother back to the house. If they had expected Miss Hardy to be frightened, the boys were doomed to disappointment. She greeted them with a scornful sniff. "Humph! Nothing but a moth-eaten dummy. I suspected as much."

Joe burst out laughing. "Aw, you peeked, Aunt Gertrude!"

As he set the gorilla down on the window-seat, the brothers examined it. The stuffed animl was shabby and patches of fur were missing.

"Boy, this really is moth-eaten," Frank murmured. "You have sharp eyes, Aunty."

Aunt Gertrude pursed her lips as she resumed sweeping crumbs off the dining-room tablecloth. "Probably left over from Halloween," she snapped. "No doubt some prankster thought the creature would have me screaming my head off."

"He should have known better." Joe winked at his brother. "Odd sort of a prank, though. Maybe one of the high school crowd got hold of a stuffed ape."

Frank gave a puzzled shrug. "I don't recall hearing any of our gang mention one. It could have been an outsider."

Both boys loved nothing better than a spine-tingling mystery. Their father, Fenton Hardy, a former New York police detective, was now a private investigator in the coastal town of Bayport. His success in cracking difficult cases had won him a nationwide reputation. Frank and Joe often helped on his assignments and also had solved several baffling cases on their own, starting with *The Mystery of the Aztec Warrior*.

"Look," Joe proposed. "You don't suppose this could have been left by one of Dad's enemies – maybe as a warning the house is being watched?"

"It's possible," Frank said doubtfully.

Mr Hardy had flown to Europe on a secret government assignment, and the boys' mother was away visiting relatives. In their absence, Aunt Gertrude was keeping house for her nephews.

"Now don't you two go looking for trouble with dangerous criminals," she warned. "You've been mixed up in enough mysteries. Mark my words, you'll bring on a real calamity one of these days!"

Though fond of making dire predictions, their Aunt Gertrude was secretly thrilled over the family's detective exploits.

"Okay, we'll watch our step," Joe promised.

"Speaking of mysteries, Joe," said Frank, "let's see if we can pick up any more of that scrambled broadcast."

As the boys headed for the hall stairway, Miss Hardy's scolding voice followed them. "And take this nasty fake ape with you – or at least get it out of the dining-room!"

Grinning, Joe went back to retrieve the gorilla. In the attic, the boys heard only light static trickling from the speaker. Both hunched over the short-wave rig as Frank played the dial back and forth.

The boys's radio gear for their station – a separate unit from the set in Mr Hardy's study – was arrayed on a long table. It included a receiver, a transceiver with VOX hookup, a signal generator, and a phone patch. The transmitter for the main rig was mounted on a relay rack next to the table. On the wall above hung two framed General Class licenses, several award certificates, and a flag-pinned world map. Another wall was papered with rows of colourful QSL cards – acknowledgments of the boys' contacts with hams all over the world.

"Guess we've lost it," Frank said, after trying vainly to bring in the scrambled broadcast.

"I'd sure like to know where that came from," Joe

said. "No ordinary ham would have any reason for using a scrambler."

"Or any *right* to, for that matter," Frank, who was twirling the dial, paused in surprise as a grim, rasping voice blurted out of the speaker:

"*Apeman calling the Hardys! Apeman calling the Hardys! Do you read me?*"

Frank flashed a startled look at the stuffed gorilla, then grabbed the microphone. 'Apeman from WBE2XEJ! . . . What is all this?'

In response came a series of deep-throated snorts and growls. Then the voice resumed:" *This is the only warning you'll get, Hardys! My agent is watching the house and I have ordered him to – *" More snorts and growls followed.

"His agent!" Joe gasped. "Does he mean that gorilla?"

Before Frank could reply, the menacing sounds from the speaker gave way to wild howls of laughter! The Hardys traded looks of chagrin as both recognized their 'apeman' caller.

"Chet Morton!" Joe groaned.

Tubby, freckle-faced Chet – also a ham operator – was the Hardys' best pal, he had been an invaluable help to them on several dangerous adventures.

"WB2XEJ from W2RBR," Chet's voice came in with a sound of munching close to the microphone. "Howdy, Hardys! Thought you'd never pick me up. Was I snortin' loud and clear?"

In spite of themselves, Frank and Joe could not help laughing.

"Very funny, you big ape,' Frank said. "You really

had us going there for a while. By the way, before you eat any more monkey food, you'd better adjust your frequency."

"Oops, thanks for the tip! ... I guess you guys spotted King Kong, my secret agent."

"That mildewed ape! We sure did."

Chet explained that he had planted the gorilla in their evergreen and then had sped home in his jalopy to follow up the joke on short-wave.

"We thought that was you in the tree, at first," Joe put in, taking the mike. 'Boy, that's a real prize, Chet! Where'd you get him?"

"At the museum. Been tucked away on a storeroom shelf for umpteen years – in fact they were going to throw him out. You see, I've been studying taxidermy over there – "

"Taxidermy?' Joe echoed, grinning at Frank. The Hardys were familiar with Chet's constant mania for embarking on new hobbies.

"Sure. You know – stuffed animals. No kidding, it's real interesting!"

"I'll bet. At least it'll be a change from stuffing yourself."

"Okay, gagster. I'm serious. Matter of fact, that's the main reason I called. How about you guys coming to an auction with me tomorrow?"

"What kind of auction." Joe asked.

"At the Elias Batter estate on Hill Road." Chet gave the address and said that the late owner had been an accomplished taxidermist. "Seems a lot of his stuffed specimens are being sold off with the rest of the household effects. I figure I might pick up some bargains and start a collection. Will you and Frank join me?"

"Why us?"

"I'll explain later. Come on, be a sport," Chet pleaded. "Meet you there at eleven."

Joe conferred hastily with his brother, then agreed. "Okay. Frank says maybe this taxidermy kick will keep you out of trouble with the FCC for monkey business over the air." Chuckling, Joe signed off, "So long for now, W2RBR from WB2XEJ ... and WB2XEJ is QRT."

Next day, after their Saturday morning chores, the Hardys drove to the auction. Chet's gorilla was stowed in the back of their convertible.

The Batter estate proved to be a dark old Victorian mansion, set among wide grounds fringed with oak and beech trees. A number of people were wandering about the lawn, but most of the crowd was clustered near a large stable-garage where the auctioneer had set up his platform. As Frank and Joe found a parking place at one side of the gravel driveway, they could see him holding up an elaborate lamp.

"Eight dollars, ladies and gentlemen! Do I hear a bid for nine? . . . Nine, anyone?"

"We should have brought Aunt Gertrude," Frank said. "Bet she would have loved this!"

Just then the Hardy's saw their stout chum plodding towards them, lugging a flat wooden box and a strange-looking stuffed animal. It had ears similar to a donkey's, powerfully clawed feet, and a long piggish snout.

"Hi, guys!" Chet called, "Look what I got!"

"Wow! What is *that*?" Joe gasped,

"An aardvark – an African termite-eater." Chet set down his prize proudly near the Hardy's convertible, then opened the box, displaying a set of surgical instruments inside. "And get a load of this – Batter's old taxidermist's kit! Only eight bucks for both!"

Before either Frank or Joe could comment, they heard a sudden shout, "*Thief . . . stop, thief!*"

A brown station wagon came roaring out from behind the garage and down the curving drive.

"Look out! He'll clip us!" Chet screeched. As the boys leapt aside, the Hardys glimpsed two men in the front seat – the driver was unshaven and double-chinned; the other man, thin and bald.

The station wagon was wheeling so fast it was nearly out of control. Skidding on the gravel, it sideswiped the rear bumper of the Hardy's convertible, rebounded across the drive to a tree on the other side, then zoomed out on to the roadway and sped off with a blast from the exhaust!

"Those crazy nuts!" Joe fumed.

Chet was staring wide-eyed after the station wagon. "Did you see that? It was loaded with stuffed animals!"

"Come on! After 'em!" Frank called to his brother.

Leaving Chet standing open-mouthed with his purchases, the Hardys leapt into their convertible. Frank gunned the engine to life and they roared off in pursuit of the thieves.

2

A Broken Antenna

The station wagon was nearly out of sight, but Frank pressed hard on the accelerator and gradually narrowed the distance. Far ahead, at the end of Hill Road, they saw the car turn right.

"Must be heading out of town!" Joe muttered.

The Hardys followed at top speed. Fortunately, the blacktopped highway on to which their quarry had turned was almost empty of traffic. In a few moments they again had the station wagon in view.

Joe pulled binoculars from the glove compartment, focused on the thieves' licence plate, and jotted down the number.

"They're turning again!" Frank said. The brown car shot off to the left into Barmet Woods.

As the Hardy's reached the turnoff spot, Frank spun the wheel. With a screech of tyres their convertible plunged across the road into a rutted dirt lane, winding among the trees.

"Yikes! Save the springs!" Joe exclaimed

The jolting forced Frank to slow down. In the crisp autumn air, the trees were ablaze with colour, but the Hardys were too preoccupied with the chase to enjoy the scenery. Suddenly they heard a sharp *thump* in the distance.

"What was that?" asked Joe.

"Maybe that driver hit something," Frank said.

Rounding a bend farther ahead, the boys saw a large animal lying across the road.

"It's a deer!" Joe leapt out as his brother slammed on the brakes. The creature was lying on its side with no sign of life.

"Never had a chance," Frank said grimly. Tyre marks in the dirt showed that the station wagon had backed up and steered around its victim.

As the boys dragged the deer off the road, Joe noticed a gleam of metal in the underbrush. "Hey, look!" he said, picking up a slender rod with three branching extensions. "It's the thieves' short-wave antenna!"

"You're right – I remember seeing it mounted on their front fender. Must've snapped off when their wagon hit the deer." Frank examined the find. "Never saw one like this before, did you?"

Joe shook his head. "Looks homemade to me."

"Keep it. This might be a clue," Frank advised.

The Hardys resumed the chase, but now with little hope of overtaking the culprits. A mile or more farther on, the woods ended and the dirt lane connected with a heavily travelled highway.

"Fat chance of catching them now,' Joe said. 'We don't even know which way they went.'

Frank agreed. 'The State Police should be notified,' he said.

Over the convertible's short-wave the boys transmitted an alarm to State Police headquarters. Then they stopped at the nearest gas station to phone a report of the deer accident to the local game warden, a friend of the Hardys.

By the time they returned to the Batter estate, the auction was over and most of the crowd had left. Chet was waiting patiently at the parking area, perched in his high-sprung yellow jalopy, the Queen, near a Bayport police car. In the Queen's back seat, with the aardvark and taxidermy kit, stood a black bear cub.

"What happened?" The chubby youth hopped out anxiously from behind the wheel. "Did you catch those thieves?"

Frank shook his head. "No, but we got their licence number."

"Don't tell us you added *another* prize to your collection!" Joe said, grinning at the bear cub.

"Sure, that was my first buy – before you two got here," Chet said proudly. "It was a bigger bargain than the aardvark!"

"It's big enough, all right. Where do you plan to keep this stuffed zoo of yours?"

Chet gave a slight cough. "Well, er, as a matter of fact that's why I – "

"Hold it!" Frank said. "That squad-car officer just motioned to us, Joe."

The policeman who had beckoned was conferring with the tall, dapperly dressed auctioneer and a smaller, grey-haired man near the garage-stable while another officer took notes.

The Hardys hurried over, bringing the broken antenna, and reported their fruitless chase. "Here's the licence number," Joe added, handing over the scrap of paper. "We've already alerted the highway patrol."

"Good work, boys," the policeman said. "This antenna may help us get a line on the thieves."

"We suspect it's a handmade job," Frank said. "By the way, what did they take?"

"Not much, luckily," the auctioneer replied. "Just nine stuffed animals."

"That's the strangest haul I ever heard of,' Joe put in. "Why in the world would the thieves want them?"

The aucitoneer gave a puzzled laugh. "Good question. They certainly weren't worth a lot. The bids on all nine didn't amount to more than a hundred dollars."

He explained that after being auctioned off, each item had been taken to the garage, to be claimed later by the high bidder. It was there that the grey-haired clerk had been held up.

Apparently the two thieves had arrived at the auction late, when the nine animals had already been sold but not yet picked up. The men had first offered to pay the clerk more than the amounts bid. When he refused, they had seized the animals at gunpoint and fled.

"Too bad. I hope they're caught," Joe said.

As the Hardys walked back to Chet, Frank said thoughtfully, "You know, Joe, this robbery has the makings of a real mystery. There must be *some* reason for pulling such a crazy holdup."

Joe nodded. "Unless we were chasing a couple of nuts!"

Chet was struck with a sudden idea when he heard

about the deer. "Gee, good study specimens are hard for us taxidermists to come by,' he said. "I wonder if the game warden would let me have the head for mounting."

"Probably." Frank climbed into the Hardys' convertible. "We'll call him when we get home."

"Great! But – er – what's the hurry? Wouldn't you guys like some lunch?"

"That's where we're going – home to eat."

"Come on to the Hot Rocket," Chet said, "and I'll stand treat for hamburgers and malts."

Joe looked at his brother in surprise and burst out laughing. "Wow! We don't get an offer like that every day! It's a deal, pal!"

Later, as they were finishing lunch at their high school crowd's favourite eating spot, Chet cleared his throat nervously. "Say, guys, how are you fixed for lab space at your house?"

"Lab space?" Frank raised his eyebrows.

"Uh-huh. You see, Mom's not too happy about me doing this taxidermy at home, and – well, I thought . . ." Chet's voice trailed off and he looked at his pals beseechingly.

The Hardys joined in peals of laughter.

"Now it comes out!" Joe exclaimed. "I knew there was a catch to this free lunch!"

"Not to mention inviting us to that auction!"

"I wouldn't take up much room – honest!" Chet looked so wistful that the Hardys relented.

"Well, okay, if Aunt Gertrude doesn't object," Frank said. "I guess she won't mind as long as you're working up in our garage lab."

"On second thought," Joe said with a grin, "maybe we'd better call the game warden from here, where she can't listen in. Somehow I don't think she'd care much for a deer's head."

Mr Dorsey, the warden, readily promised that Chet could pick up the head and pelt at the game reserve later that day. After Joe emerged from the phone booth, the Hardys drove home to Elm Street in their convertible, followed by Chet's backfiring jalopy.

Aunt Gertrude peered suspiciously out of a back window as the stuffed animals were being unloaded and soon emerged to give advice to the boys.

"Humph! Taxidermy, eh?" she commented. "Very well. I daresay it has some educational value. But don't let me see any messy stuffing being tracked into the house, or I'll have three scalps mounted over the door! Understand?"

"Yes, ma'am!" Chet gulped.

Frank and Joe had fitted up the entire second storey of the garage as a detective laboratory and clubhouse. Leaving Chet to arrange a working space, the Hardys hurried into the house to their father's study and checked his criminal files for pictures of the auction thieves.

"No luck," Frank said at last. "But let's keep in touch with Chief Collig on this case, Joe. I have a hunch there may be some interesting angle we don't know about yet.'

Chief Collig, a veteran of the Bayport police force, was a long-time friend of the Hardys. The two young sleuths stopped in to see him on their way back from the game reserve with Chet.

"Have you traced the auction thieves' licence number yet?" Joe inquired eagerly.

The husky officer replied with a quizzical grin, "We tried to, but we got a surprise. No licence plates with that number were ever issued. Sure you didn't read it wrong?"

"Positive! I was using binoculars."

Collig rubbed his jaw thoughtfully. "Then it sounds as if those hoods were no amateurs – not if their car's equipped with fake plates."

"What about the radio antenna?" Frank asked.

"No use. That turned out to be homemade too, as you suspected, so there's no way to trace it."

Frank had an idea. "May we have it?"

"Sure, why not?" Collig pulled the antenna from one of his desk drawers and handed it over. "Want to use it on the rig in your convertible?"

"No, but it's an odd design," Frank explained. "If Joe and I mount it on our car, it may attract attention. Someone might recognize it and give us a lead on the owner."

On Sunday, after church, Aunt Gertrude said good-bye to her nephews and went off with a ladies group to visit sick members of the congregation. The boys were alone in the house when the telephone rang. Frank answered and was delighted to hear his father's voice.

"Dad! What a swell surprise! Where are you?"

"At Bayport Airport, son. Just landed from Paris this morning and then hopped a plane from New York. Think you and Joe could pick me up?"

"You bet. We'll be there in a jiffy!"

Fifteen minutes later the tall, broad-shouldered investigator was embracing his two sons.

"Boy, you look great, Dad!" Joe said. "How'd you make out on your case in Europe?"

"Tell you about it later. Right now I could use some of Aunt Gertrude's home cooking."

"You're out of luck," Frank said. "She won't be home until three o'clock."

Mr Hardy chuckled wryly. "In that case I'll settle for ham and eggs at the nearest diner."

After stowing their father's luggage in the trunk of the convertible, the boys took him to a roadside restaurant just outside Bayport. Soon the three were settled in a comfortable booth, enjoying their meal. "Okay, let's hear about your case, Dad," Frank urged.

Mr Hardy explained that he had been investigating the theft of secret data from a California aircraft company. Certain features of its latest commercial jet plane had been copied by two European firms. "A clear case of industrial espionage," the detective went on. "And some of those features are usable on military aircraft."

"Any clues?" Joe asked.

"Just one, so far. The gang that peddled the data uses 'aardvark' as a code word."

"Aardvark?" Frank echoed. He glanced at Joe and both laughed. "There's a funny coincidence! Chet Morton bought a stuffed one yesterday."

"What's Chet up to now?" Mr Hardy inquired.

Before Frank could reply, Joe bolted from his seat with a startled gasp.

"Hey! What's wrong?" Frank asked.

"That bald auction thief!" Joe exclaimed, pointing out the window. "I just saw him out there on the parking lot!"

3

Ghost Light

Frank sprang up at Joe's mention of the auction thief, and both boys dashed to the door. A stout couple were entering the restaurant. Joe tried to skid aside, but Frank barged into him and they collided heavily with the man and woman.

"Well, of all the fresh young ruffians!" The woman glared at the two boys as she tried to straighten her hat which had been knocked askew in the impact.

"We're terribly sorry, ma'am," Frank apologized. "My brother just spotted a thief on the parking lot – we were running out to catch him!"

"Er, better stand aside, dear!" the woman's husband said hastily as he saw tall, husky Fenton Hardy striding to join the two youths.

"Please excuse my sons," the detective said.

As the woman gave a mollified smile, the Hardys squeezed past her. Outside, Joe gazed around, then exclaimed, "There he goes!"

A thin, baldheaded figure in a flapping tan raincoat was sprinting off the lot.

A green sedan was waiting at the edge of the highway, engine racing. The baldheaded man leapt into it. Joe, Frank, and Mr Hardy were still weaving their way among the parked cars when the sedan roared off into the stream of traffic. There was no chance to note its licence number.

"Rats!" Joe panted. "We lost 'em again!"

"Did you notice that fat-necked thug at the wheel?" Frank said.

"I sure did – he's the same man who was driving the station wagon yesterday!"

"Suppose you two fill me in," said Mr Hardy.

The boys related their adventure at the auction.

"Maybe we ought to check our convertible," Frank added.

"Just what I was thinking," Joe said. "I have a hunch Baldy may have been tampering with it."

"The Hardys hurried towards their car. Frank exclaimed as they reached it, "Look! The antenna's gone – that's what he was after!"

The thieves' odd-shaped short-wave antenna, which the boys had mounted on their convertible, was now missing.

Mr Hardy frowned. "Rather odd to encounter those two again the very next day. Did you tell anyone about coming to met me?"

Frank shook his head. "Nobody. When you called, we jumped into the car and took off."

"Maybe they were just driving along the highway and spotted the antenna on our car," Joe suggested.

"What was the baldheaded guy doing when you noticed him?" Frank asked.

Joe gave a shrug. "I couldn't see well enough to tell. A car drove up and blocked my view."

On a hunch, Frank walked around to the trunk.

"Oh, oh! Look here!" He pointed to some bright metal scratches around the keyhole.

"Looks as if he tried to jimmy it!" Joe said.

"Better unlock the trunk, Frank, and see if anything else is missing," Mr Hardy advised.

Frank did so. Neither his father's suitcases nor the briefcase had been disturbed.

"Guess the guy didn't have time to finish breaking in," Frank said, closing the trunk lid.

"Carrying anything valuable, Dad?" Joe asked.

"Not especially – except for my case reports. They deal with the aircraft theft and several other recent industrial espionage cases. I've a theory they're all the work of the same gang."

Frank and Joe exchanged glances.

"If Baldy was after one of those case reports," Joe reasoned, "he may be one of the gang!"

"It's a possibility," his father agreed.

That afternoon Chet Morton dropped over to work on his taxidermy project, and again the next day Frank and Joe saw the light burning in the garage crime lab when they arrived home from school.

"Boy, I guess Chet's really serious about this taxidermy kick,' Joe remarked.

After putting down their books and washing their hands, Frank and Joe went to the kitchen for a snack.

"I'm afraid Chester is missing meals and living on grapefruit out in your lab," Aunt Gertrude fretted.

"Grapefruit?" Frank murmured, pouring milk.

"Yes, he borrowed a knife from me yesterday. It's not good for him, not getting a well-balanced diet. You'd better take him out a sandwich."

"Good idea. We'll see how he's making out."

The Hardys found Chet hunched over an array of chemical bottles, tools, a bag of salt, and a nearly finished stuffed squirrel which he was preparing for a high school exhibit.

"How's it going, Chet?" Frank asked, handing him the sandwich.

"Oh, swell! The deer's already at the tanner's, and I've ordered a head form from Roundtree's shop. Did the skin-fleshing myself."

"So I see," Joe said, picking up a soiled grapefruit knife. "Did you flesh it with this?"

"Yes, your aunt lent it to me." Seeing the Hardys' expressions, Chet's eyes widened innocently. "Do you think she'll mind? Gee, it's for a scientific cause!"

Frank nudged his brother, then looked threateningly at Chet. "Morton, old boy, if we find deer meat in our grapefruit tomorrow morning, we'll personally stuff you."

"With breakfast? You've got a deal!"

Joe threw up his arms. "We can't win!"

A shrill summons from Aunt Gertrude brought the Hardys hurrying back to the house. "A man wants to speak to you two on the phone," she reported. "Says his name's Crowell – J. Sylvester Crowell."

Joe looked at his brother blankly as they strode towards the hall telephone and muttered, "Wonder who he is."

When Frank answered, Crowell explained that he was the attorney for the wife of the late Elias Batter. "Mr Batter has asked me to thank you boys for your efforts to catch those thieves who stole the stuffed animals," Crowell went on. "We understand you two are already following in your father's footsteps – as detectives, I mean."

"We've solved a few cases," Frank admitted.

"Well, even though you're amateurs, she thought you might like to undertake a little more – shall we say, practice work at detecting?"

"Such as?" Frank inquired cautiously.

"She herself will tell you all about it. Could you come to my office in half an hour?"

Joe, who was listening in, nodded eagerly.

"We'll be there," Frank told the lawyer.

Crowell proved to be a balding, long-nosed man in a pinstripe suit. He introduced the boys to a short, dowdily dressed woman. "Mrs Batter, I'd like to present Frank and Joe Hardy."

She nodded curtly without offering her hand and looked the boys over appraisingly.

"We didn't realize Mr Batter was married," Frank said. "We thought since his estate was being auctioned off – "

"No sense in living in that draughty old mausoleum!" she snapped. "Just a white elephant, that's all it is. How would I keep it up? Elias left me barely enough to live on as it is!"

"That's why Mrs Batter is eager to recover those stolen animals," Crowell put in smoothly. "Every penny counts, you see."

"What he means," the widow said bluntly, "is that I have no money to waste on fancy detective agency fees. Now, you two boys are smart young fellows I hear. Would you take on the job of tracking down those thieves and getting back my property for me?"

"We never charge for our services, if that's what you mean," Frank said. "Joe and I aren't professional detectives."

"Good! Then you'll take the case. Maybe your father would even be willing to help."

Frank smiled. "If he does, he'll charge." Frank was amused at the woman's stingy eagerness to get as much work as possible free. "Besides, Dad's tied up on another case. But my brother and I will do what we can."

"Have you any idea why the stuffed animals were taken?" Joe asked.

Mrs Batter's beady green eyes glared suspiciously at the younger Hardy boy. "To sell for whatever they bring, I suppose. Why else?"

"But the auctioneer said the thieves first offered to buy them," Joe reminded her. "And for a higher price than was bid."

There was brief silence. Then Crowell cleared his throat. "Well, perhaps the thieves were collectors – or thought the animals were more valuable than they really are. At any rate, Mrs Batter wants her property back, no matter how little it's worth. As I said, every penny counts." He flashed the boys a toothy smile.

"Did Mr Batter have any friends who might know more about those animals?" Frank asked.

Mrs Batter sniffed. "I had nothing to do with Elias's friends – or his business affairs."

"What *was* his business?" Joe inquired.

"Investments. That's all he ever told *me*. They didn't amount to much, I can tell you that!"

Driving home, Frank mused aloud, "If you ask me, Mrs Batter knows more than she's telling."

Joe nodded. "I got the same impression. But where do we start on this case?"

"Remember how the thieves' station wagon side-swiped our car and then struck a tree when they were making their getaway?"

"Sure. What about it?"

"There might be some paint flecks in the tree bark,' Frank reasoned. "And if the wagon ever had a repaint job, those particles might help us trace the garage where it was done."

"Swell idea!" Joe said. "That brown colour didn't look as if it were the original shade."

Not until after supper were the Hardys able to drive out to the Batter estate. The high, gabled mansion loomed starkly against the sky, silvered by moonlight. A broken porch rail and dark, blank windows gave it a sinister look.

"Spooky-looking layout," Joe muttered. "It's a cinch no one's taking care of the place."

Beaming flashlights, the boys carefully examined the tree which had been hit by the thieves' car. To their disappointment, the only mark was low on the trunk, about two feet from the ground.

Frank sighed. "I guess we're out of luck."

"Looks that way," Joe agreed. "They must have just grazed it with their front bumper. And their tyre tracks don't – " He broke off as Frank suddenly clutched his arm. "What's the matter?"

"Take a look!" Frank pointed to the house.

A faint glow of light could be seen moving about inside the front windows!

·4·

Irate Stranger

Joe was as startled as his brother by the eerie light in the mansion. "Oh, oh! Maybe this trip wasn't so useless after all!" he whispered.

"Come on! Let's find out what gives!" Frank urged.

Switching off their flashlights, the young sleuths darted across the lawn.

"Watch it!" Joe warned suddenly. "Whoever's in there may be coming out!"

The light was moving towards the front door. Both boys dived for cover among the bushes surrounding the porch. A moment later the door creaked open. A small figure stepped out and clicked the lock shut behind him.

Frank and Joe peered cautiously from the bushes. To their amazement, the mansion's mysterious visitor was a boy, about eleven or twelve years old!

"Just a kid," Joe muttered. Feelling a bit foolish, the Hardys rose from their hiding place.

The boy gave a screech of fright and leapt down the porch steps in a wild dash for safety. Frank and Joe grabbed him before he had gone more than a few yards.

"Sorry if we scared you," Frank said. "We just want to know what you were doing in there."

Joe switched on his flashlight for a beter look at
their captive. The boy was freckle-faced, thin, and
shivering, clad in a threadbare sweater, dirty jeans,
and tennis shoes.

"What's it to you what I was doing?" he retorted
defiantly. "And stop blinding me with that light, wise
guy!"

"Okay. Simmer down, pal." The chuckle left Joe's
voice as he went on, "We could call the police, you
know, if you'd rather – Oof!"

Lowering his head suddenly, the boy had butted
Joe in the midriff! As Joe staggered back, the youngster made another break for freedom, but again Frank
seized him. The boy flailed his fists, punching wildly,
but the Hardys managed to pinion his arms.

"Wow! You pack a mean wallop in those knuckles!"
Frank said, smiling.

Joe added soothingly, "Just take it easy now. We're
not going to hurt you."

"Then stop talking about calling the cops!"

"All right. Fair enough." Frank relaxed his hold.
"I'm Frank Hardy, by the way, and this is my brother
Joe. What's your name?"

The boy hesitated, then muttered, "Jimmy."

"Jimmy what?"

"Jimmy Batter."

"*Batter?*" exclaimed Joe. "You mean you're related
to the man who owned this house?"

"Sure. He was my uncle – Uncle Elly."

Frank and Joe exchanged thoughtful glances in the
moonlit darkness. "What were you doing here,
Jimmy?"

The boy shrugged. "Just looking around."

"What for?"

"For nothing!" Jimmy flared. "Does there have to be a reason? Uncle Elly was good to me, that's all. I – I just wanted to get another look at the place before it's sold."

"Did Mrs Batter know you were coming?" Frank persisted. "I mean your aunt."

"Naw. Neither does my ma. She wouldn't have anything to do with Uncle Elly, and she didn't like me seeing him, either. That's why I had to sneak over after dark."

"How did you get in?" asked Joe.

"Jimmy produced a key. "Uncle Elly gave it to me. He liked to have me come and visit him, especially after he got laid up in bed."

Frank rubbed his jaw, considering. The boy's story seemed plausible, but Frank was not altogether convinced. Nor was Joe. Both felt Jimmy might be holding back something.

"How much longer are you guys going to keep me here?" the boy complained. "I answered your questions, didn't I?"

"Yes, you did," Frank admitted. There was something appealing about the small, undernourished youngster, shivering in the autumn darkness. "Look. Jimmy! How'd you like to come home with us for some sandwiches and cocoa?"

Jimmy stared in surprise. "What's the catch?"

"No catch," Joe said. "We're kind of hungry, after the workout you gave us. How about you?"

"Guess I wouldn't mind. Where do you live?"

"Elm Street. That's our convertible parked down there on the drive."

Jimmy gave an admiring whistle. "Hey! Pretty keen!"

"We have a ham radio setup, too," Frank added persuasively. "You can listen in, if you like."

"All right. I'll come along." Jimmy's bored, casual tone of voice made both Hardys grin.

When they reached home, Frank and Joe found that Aunt Gertrude had retired early. "Guess we'll have to rustle up our own snacks," Frank said. He heated cups of cocoa while Joe made man-sized ham sandwiches.

Jimmy ate so ravenously that the Hardys wondered when he had last had a decent meal. "Boy, this is a swell house!" the youngster said, looking around the cheerful kitchen.

When the snack was finished and Jimmy had stuffed his pocket with cookies, Frank and Joe asked if he would like to see their short-wave rig. The youngster's thin face lit up. "Sure!"

They climbed the stairs to the attic radio shack. Jimmy watched, wide-eyed, as the older boys warmed up their set, then picked up and responded to a couple of distant hums. Feeling they had won the youngster's confidence, Joe began questioning him again about his visit to Elias Batter's mansion.

At once Jimmy's expression changed. "None of your business!" he blurted. "Don't think you can con me with any free handout – I knew all along there was some catch to it!" He darted for the stairway. Joe sprang up to follow.

Frank had been turning the dial. He was about to join Joe in pursuit of the youngster when both boys froze as a voice crackled from the radio:

"*Aardvark bulldog . . . Aardvark bulldog . . .*"

"Aardvark!" Frank echoed with a startled glance at Joe.

"The code name Dad told us about!" As Joe spoke, a loud volley of barks came over the speaker.

Then the voice resumed, droning out a strange flow of words and numbers. Grabbing a pencil, Frank jotted them down:

7 2 PROGRESS SHEEP   3 4 ACTIVITIES
1 1 FLIGHT HAIRS.

After a pause, the voice repeated the message. Again came a sound of barking. Then silence.

"Jumpin' catfish!" Joe gasped. "Do you suppose that was the gang?"

"Could be. It certainly was a code of some kind – and that means whoever sent it much have some reason for keeping the message secret."

"If only Dad were home!" said Joe. "Think he'll be in tonight?"

Frank shook his head. "When we shoved off for school this morning, he told me he was flying to New York and wouldn't be home until tomorrow."

'Try calling him at his usual hotel," Joe suggested. "I'll check on Jimmy."

The boys hurried downstairs. There was no sign of their freckle-faced guest, but Joe found the front door ajar. Evidently Jimmy had failed to slam it tight when he stormed out.

Frank, meanwhile, put through a long-distance call to New York and succeeded in contacting their father. Mr Hardy received the report on the code message with keen interest.

"The 'aardvark bulldog' part must represent the thieves' call signs," he said thoughtfully.

"Right, Dad. And the barking could be the response, indicating that contact has been made or the message has been received," Frank declared.

"It may take a good bit of work to crack the message itself," the detective went on. "See what you two can do with it, and we'll talk more tomorrow when I get home."

The Hardy boys pored over the message a while, then belatedly tackled their homework. Finally, as a swelling patter of rain outside caused them both to yawn drowsily, they went to bed.

Next day when they arrived home from school, Frank said, "I've been thinking, Joe – maybe we ought to check that story Jimmy told us."

"Wouldn't hurt. What do you have in mind?"

"Well, for one thing, I'd like to know if he really is Elias Batter's nephew."

The Hardys checked the Bayport telephone directory. The only Batter listed was the late Elias Batter. Frank dialled the attorney, J. Sylvester Crowell, and asked if Elias had had a nephew.

"Why, yes – a boy named Gordon, Jimmy Gordon," Crowell replied. "His mother is Elias Batter's sister. She's a widow. Why do you ask?"

"We met Jimmy and just wanted to be sure who he

is," Frank said guardedly. "Could you give me Mrs Gordon's full name and address?"

After jotting down the information, Frank hung up with a frown. "So we know Jimmy lied to us about his last name, at least."

"That's not surprising," Joe said. "He was probably worried we might get in touch with his mother and tell on him."

Aunt Gertrude had gone out to visit a neighbour. The boys raided the cookie jar, then went up to their room, intending to resume work on the code message. Joe saw his brother glance sharply out the window.

"What's the matter?" Joe inquired.

"There's a man down in the yard. We'd better go see what he wants."

The brothers hurried downstairs again and out of the back door. A tall, gaunt man, rather seedily dressed in a snap-brim hat and checked topcoat, was peering into the garage.

"Want something?" Frank asked.

The man seemed startled, but he spoke truculently. "You two are the Hardy boys?" Frank nodded. "And you killed a deer the other day?"

"We didn't kill it," Joe said. "We found it dead on the road. Someone else – "

"Don't give me that!" The gaunt man glowered at them. "I got evidence you punks ran it down. That was my pet deer – '

"Your deer!" Frank exclaimed, astonished.

"That's right. I raised it from a fawn. You two even took the head and pelt." The man's narrow eyes roved around the yard and squinted at the house windows. "I aim to find them."

"Just a minute!" Frank blocked the intruder's path. "I haven't heard of any 'pet' deer running loose in Barmet Woods."

"Well, you're hearing about it now! That deer was worth at least sixty dollars to me, but if you'll pay for it, I won't make any trouble."

"We're not paying anything," Joe said firmly.

The man hesitated. "Make it thirty, then. I wouldn't want to see you fellows go to jail. But if I have to call the police – "

"We'll call them ourselves," Frank broke in. "What's your name, mister?"

"Now hold on. Let's cool down, buddy. No sense asking for a lot of bad publicity." The man's voice became frankly wheedling. "Make it twenty and we'll call it quits. You kids can afford that. Do you work after school?" Again the stranger peered around inquisitively.

"Never mind about us," Frank said. "We didn't kill the deer and we won't pay a cent. What's more, you'd better tell us who you are and what you're doing here."

"Smart alecks, eh?" The man's bony, long-nosed face twisted with anger. Shaking his fist, he turned down the driveway. "You haven't heard the last of this. I gave you a chance to stay out of trouble. Now you'll have to settle the hard way!"

Alley Escape

Frank and Joe stared after the gaunt stranger as he strode off down the driveway.

"You don't suppose he can really make any trouble for us, do you?" Joe muttered.

"Of course not," Frank scoffed. "Our front end isn't dented and we reported the accident. That guy's just a phony!"

"Sure, but if it comes to a showdown, we can't prove it wasn't our car that hit the deer."

"I think the game warden knows us well enough to take our word. But let's find out."

The boys hurried back into the house. Mr Dorsey, the game warden, snorted angrily when Frank telephoned and told of their caller. "If that fellow's story were true, *he'd* be in trouble with the law. Around here it's illegal for a private owner to keep a wild deer as a pet. Just send the man to me if he bothers you again."

"We sure will," Frank said gratefully. "What I'd like to know is how he got our names."

Dorsey explained that he had had a call about the deer on Saturday night. "I thought it was some indignant wildlife lover, but it could've been the same fellow. Said he'd seen the dead deer earlier and wondered if some poacher had got it. I told him you boys had reported the accident, and I'd given you and your chum the head and pelt." The warden added, "Sorry it led to you two being annoyed."

"That's all right," Frank said. "We just wanted to check up on the guy."

Joe chuckled in relief after hearing what the warden said. "Just a shakedown artist, eh?"

At that moment the boys heard their names shouted from the back yard. "There's Chet," said Frank. "Wonder what's up."

The Hardys went through the kitchen and out of the door to meet their friend.

Chet, who was carrying his stuffed squirrel, greeted them with an embarrassed look. "Say, guys, we really goofed on that deer. He belonged to somebody!"

"What do you mean?" Joe blurted.

"I just met the owner out front. Seems the deer was his pet. He was pretty mad but I – "

Frank grabbed Chet's shoulder. 'You didn't give him any money?"

"Ten dollars," Chet said, shrugging. "The head was worth that much to me. He wanted more, but I talked him down to ten."

Joe groaned. "Chet, you've been swindled!"

"Swindled?" Chet's jaw dropped and he stared at the Hardys. "How come?"

"That guy didn't own the deer – he's just a con man," Frank explained. "He tried to shake us down, too, but we called his bluff."

"Why, that low-down cheat!" Chet's moonface turned beet-red with anger. Dropping his stuffed squirrel, he bounded off down the driveway. "He's not getting away with my ten bucks!"

Half startled, half amused, Frank and Joe ran after their friend. Far ahead on Elm Street, more than a block away, they could make out a tall, shuffling figure.

"That's the man!" Chet yelled. Spurred by anger, he and the Hardys sprinted in pursuit.

The clatter of their leather-soled shoes reached the stranger's ears. He glanced back, then broke into a run. The chase was on!

Frank and Joe quickly drew ahead of their puffing, chunky pal, but the gaunt swindler's long-legged strides kept him a safe distance from his pursuers.

Reaching Oak Avenue, which was lined with stores, he turned right and disappeared from view. The three boys rounded the corner moments later, straining for a glimpse of their quarry. Oak Avenue led into Bayport's business district and the sidewalk was dotted with pedestrians.

"There he goes!" Frank yelled, pointing down the street.

Three blocks later, after a maddening halt by traffic en route, the boys saw the swindler dart into an alleyway between two rows of buildings.

"Now we've got him!" Chet panted.

Weaving their way through the sidewalk throng, the trio reached the alley opening. But as they plunged into the narrow passage, they collided full tilt with three small boys who were running out.

The swindler got away!

"Why don't you watch where you're going, fatso!" one of the boys yelled at Chet.

"Jimmy Gordon!" Joe exclaimed, catching the boy's arm. Jimmy angrily threw off his grasp.

"Hold 'em! Hold those kids!" came a shout from somewhere farther along the alley. The Hardys saw Policeman Con Riley, an old acquaintance, lumbering towards them through the passage.

"What's the matter?" Frank asked impatiently as he and Joe restrained the three urchins.

"I'm running those brats in!" Riley roared. "They've been marking windows, and racing carts in the supermarket. Now they're going to the station house!"

"Never mind all that. We'll be responsible for them," Joe said. "Help us catch a real crook!"

"Real crook?" Riley looked startled. "What're you talking about?"

"A swindler – he gypped me out of ten bucks," Chet complained. "He's a tall, bony guy in a checked coat. We saw him run down this alley."

"No one came out of this alley. I'd have seen him," Riley declared.

"Then he must've gone into one of these stores – through the back way," Frank said.

"That's right, he did," piped up one of Jimmy Gordon's companions. "We saw a guy like that go in the back door of the five-and-ten."

Riley glowered at the three urchins, then looked up at the Hardys and Chet. "All right, let's find him. But hang on to those litle brats -- I'm not through with 'em!"

"Okay, Jimmy – you and your pals come along and help us," Frank ordered. "And no tricks! We know your name's Jimmy Gordon and we have your address, if you try giving us the slip."

Jimmy gasped in dismay, then sullenly motioned his companions to do as Frank said. The Hardys and Chet each kept a hand on one of the smaller boys as the whole group crowded into the five-and-ten and spread out through the aisles. The gaunt swindler, however, had vanished. Policeman Riley questioned several clerks as well as pedestrians outside, and other stores in the block were also combed, but their quarry was nowhere in sight.

"Guess you're out of luck, Chet," Joe said as they collected in a group again.

"Great!" Chet groaned. "Ten bucks gone. Think of the hamburgers that would've bought!"

"You're telling us," one of the urchins said wistfully. "I could sure use one right now."

"We might've earned a handout at the hot-dog drive-in stand if that cop hadn't shown," Jimmy grumbled.

Riley gave a snort. "*Earn* a handout? That'll be the day, any time you sidewalk cowboys do a lick of honest work! Just wait till the sergeant hears what you've been up to!"

"If they're hungry," Frank said diplomatically, "why not let them go home for a decent meal? We'll take them – it's almost suppertime."

"Not for us it ain't," Jimmy muttered.

"Why not?"

"My ma doesn't get home from work till after eight.

Mike and Tommy have to get their own meals, too –
when they get 'em at all."

Frank was taken aback. He drew Policeman Riley
aside and whispered earnestly.

Riley nodded. "Okay, I'll give 'em a break this
time."

"Thanks a lot." Frank then made for a nearby
telephone booth and dialled the Hardys' number.
Aunt Gertrude, who by now had returned home,
answered his call.

At first, when Frank suggested bringing the street
waifs home to dinner, she was horrified. But after he
had explained the situation, Miss Hardy softened.
"Humph! Well, of course, if they're really hungry,
that's different. I'll set some extra places."

The youngsters looked flabbergasted at Frank's
invitation. Mike, a happy-go-lucky type with tousled
black hair, and Tommy, scrawny, with big blue eyes,
seemed ready to accept, but both glanced at Jimmy
before speaking. Evidently he was the ringleader.

"What's the catch?" Jimmy demanded gruffly.

Frank rumpled his hair. "Stop looking for catches,
wise guy. Here's a chance for some free chow. Better
take it."

"Well . . . okay."

At the Hardy house, Aunt Gertrude took one
shocked look at the dirty urchins, then set her jaw
firmly. "March them right up to the bathroom and
get them cleaned up!" she ordered. "Soap and plenty
of hot water – but don't use the good guest towels!
Chet, you're staying too, of course, so you can help."

Grinning, the older boys obeyed. By the time dinner

was served, their three young charges had been scrubbed until they glowed, and their hair combed neatly. Mr Hardy, meanwhile, had arrived from the airport. He was somewhat astonished at the array of guests but made no comment.

When Aunt Gertrude saw how the youngsters, once their shyness had worn off, attacked their plates of delicious hot roast beef and mashed potatoes, she beamed with pride. "Well," she murmured across the table to her brother, "at least they know what to do with good food."

Later, as they waited for Miss Hardy to serve dessert, the detective said to Frank and Joe:

"The FBI's becoming more and more concerned about these industrial thefts. That code message you picked up may be a real lead. Before we talk about it, though, how are you two crook chasers making out on the Batter case?"

Mr Hardy's words seemed to have an electric effect on Jimmy Gordon. His eyes blazed. "Crook-chasers? Batter case?" He glared at Frank and Joe. "So it's just like I thought – you two are nothing but stooges for the cops!"

Almost knocking over his chair, he sprang up and darted for the door with a wave to Mike and Tommy. "Come on! This whole deal's some kind of dirty frame-up! Scram, guys, scram!"

·6·

Tip-off Note

The Hardy boys acted fast and managed to restrain Mike and Tommy before they could leave the table. But Jimmy was already streaking into the hallway. Aunt Gertrude, however, had heard the uproar from the kitchen and took prompt action.

She darted into the hall, snatched an umbrella from the closet, and charged after him. As Jimmy yanked open the front door, she snagged his arm with the crook of the umbrella.

"Stop right there, young man! I want to have a word with you!"

Jimmy was about to flare back, but one glimpse of Aunt Gertrude's wrathful expression changed his mind. "Let me go!" he whined.

"Don't talk back to me, you imp! Just where did you leave your manners? Get to the table this instant!"

There was a chuckle from Fenton Hardy. "Better do as she says."

Scowling, with his lower lip out thrust, Jimmy plodded sullenly back to the dining room.

"Sorry if I frightened you lads," Mr Hardy said, resuming his place at the table. "Didn't Frank and Joe mention that I'm a private investigator?" The youngsters shook their heads.

"And the Batter case has nothing to do with you, Jimmy," put in Frank. "Your aunt asked Joe and me to recover some stuffed animals that were stolen from the auction at your uncle's place."

Jimmy gave the Hardy boys a surprised stare. "Is that why you were nosing around out there?"

"Right," Joe acknowledged. "The thieves' getaway car grazed a tree and we were checking the bark for paint traces."

"Hey! That's keen!" said Mike.

Tommy murmured, "Private eyes!" His blue ones were big with amazement.

"Now that that's settled, let's get on with the apple pie à la mode," Frank said, grinning.

By the time dessert was finished, even Jimmy looked relaxed and heaved a deep sigh of satisfaction. Chet took the youngsters out to his taxidermy workshop and offered to give them lessons in preparing stuffed animals. All three promised to come back the next day. "You can help me mount my deer's head, too," Chet added.

"My uncle Elly did a lot of that kind of work," Jimmy said. "There's still some stuffed animals over at the house." Frank and Joe traded startled looks.

Chet finally left in his jalopy. Jimmy and his two pals got into the Hardy boys' convertible and were driven home.

After Mike and Tommy had been dropped at their doors, Jimmy murmured:

"That guy you were chasing today – I know him."

"You *know* him?" Joe exclaimed in surprise.

Jimmy nodded. "I got a look at his face when he

ran in the ten-cent store. His name's Moran – Soapy
Moran. He used to work for Uncle Elly."

"What sort of work?" Frank asked.

"Nothing much – odd jobs, running errands."

A moment later Jimmy pointed ahead to a shabby
tenement building. "Here's my place."

The convertible drew up to the curb and the freckle-
faced boy climbed out. Frank said, "Will your mother
be home by now?"

"Sure, the light's on, up there in our window.
Thanks for the swell feed."

Joe waved. "Don't mention it. See you tomorrow!"

As the brothers drove off, Joe turned to Frank.
"Does it strike you as odd that this Soapy Moran
should have been connected with Elias Batter?"

"It sure does," Frank agreed. "I'd say it's no
coincidence. That whole business about the dead deer
may have been just a cover-up."

"A cover-up for what?"

Frank shook his head helplessly. "Search me.
Maybe just an excuse for snooping around our place."

Joe gave a startled whistle. "If you're right, then he
may be a member of the gang – or at least a pal of
those two auction thieves!"

"Could be. And speaking of the auction thieves, do
you remember what Jimmy said about more stuffed
animals at the house?"

"Yes, I've been wondering about them. Seems
funny they weren't auctioned off."

"Not only that," Frank pointed out, "but the thieves
may not even know about them. If we could see them,

they might give us a clue to what was so valuable about the other animals – the ones that were stolen."

Joe was excited over this possibility. "Let's drive out to Batter's house right now and take a look at them. We could borrow Jimmy's key."

"I think we should get permission first."

"Okay, let's stop somewhere and phone. We can probably find Crowell's home number in the book."

Frank parked the car at the drugstore and the two boys hurried to a telephone booth inside. Leafing through the Bayport directory, they soon found the attorney's residential listing.

Crowell was unexpectedly cool to the idea of the Hardys paying an unsupervised visit to the mansion. "I'm afraid I couldn't take responsibility for that," he said. "Mrs Batter would have to be consulted."

"Perhaps I could call her," Frank suggested. "Is she still living in Bayport?"

"Yes, in a small apartment. But right now she's out of town. Suppose I ask her as soon as she returns and then get in touch with you."

Joe's face showed disappointment when he heard the news. "Did Crowell explain why some of the animals weren't sold?"

"He said they were all supposed to be included in the auction, but a few hadn't been brought out of the house yet when the theft occurred. Right after that, Mrs Batter gave orders not to sell the rest of them."

"Sounds as if she got the same idea we did."

As the boys returned to their car, Joe said, "Hey, what's that on the windshield?"

A piece of paper had been slipped under the wiper.

Frank pulled it out. The paper bore a penciled message:

BROWN STATION WAGON DITCHED OFF
HORTON RD. $\frac{1}{4}$ ML. E. OF ROCKCREST DRIVE

"Wow! A tip-off on the thieves' getaway car!" Joe exclaimed.

"Maybe and maybe not," Frank said cautiously.

"Think it's phony?"

"Depends on where it came from." Both boys glanced up and down the street. No pedestrians were in sight on the block. "Someone may have been trailing us before we went in the drugstore," Frank conjectured.

"Well, there's one way to find out if this note's on the level," said Joe, "and that is to ride to the spot and see. We can notify the police on the way."

"Okay, let's go!"

As the convertible sped in the direction of Horton Drive, Joe radioed the Bayport police.

"Roger! I'll send a car to meet you there," the police operator responded after taking down the location.

Horton Road ran through the hills west of Bayport. Sparsely travelled at night, it connected with several of the busier highways. As they passed Rockcrest Drive, Frank slowed so they could keep a lookout for the abandoned station wagon. The hillside rose steeply on their right, while to the left of the road the ground fell away in a brush-clad slope.

"There it is!" Frank said, slamming on the brakes.

In the moonlight they could see the getaway car

clearly. It lay on a broad rocky shelf jutting out from the slope below them, its nose rammed against a tree.

The Hardys took flashlights, piled out of their convertible, and ran to the edge of the road. A swath had been battered through the high brush – evidently marking the course of the station wagon as it hurtled down the slope.

Joe plunged recklessly forward, then exclaimed, "Oops!" and almost went sprawling.

"Hey, watch it!" Frank cautioned, following more slowly. "Think you're a mountain goat?"

"I tripped on a vine or something," Joe said.

The boys proceeded, shining their flashlights ahead. As they reached the shelf, the rays of their flashlights revealed a large metal drum in the back of the station wagon. A vague feeling of alarm prickled Frank's scalp. He clutched Joe's arm.

"What's the matter?"

"Don't know exactly, but I don't like the looks of that drum" Frank said. "You sure that was a *vine* you tripped over?"

"How do I know? What difference does it make?" Joe returned impatiently.

"Plenty, maybe. That could've been a trip wire for a delayed-action fuse!" As he spoke, Frank's fear swelled to panic. "Come on! Let's get back up on the road and wait for the police!"

Yanking Joe's arm, he scrambled up the slope. They had taken only a few paces when a loud *whoomp* rent the air.

A huge pillar of fire shot up, engulfing the whole station wagon!

Wolf's Trail

Heat searing their backs, Frank and Joe clambered up to the road. Then they turned for a moment and peered below, shielding their eyes from the blaze. The station wagon was barely visible in the roaring orange column of flames.

"Jumpin' Jupiter!" Joe gasped. "We'd have been fried to a crisp if you hadn't stopped us!"

"Come on! Get back!" Frank warned curtly. "That brush is blazing!"

The fire was sweeping up the slope, reddening their faces in its glow. Frank backed their convertible out of range, deftly made a U-turn in the narrow roadway, and drove the car a safe distance away. Joe, meanwhile, radioed a fresh report to the police.

A squad car soon arrived, followed by a fire crew. Fortunately the blaze was already burning itself out, checked by the wetness of the brush from the previous night's rain.

Chief Collig had come in the squad car. "Lucky you lads got away in time," he observed.

"It sure was," Joe said. "There must have been gasoline in that drum, and some sort of electrical sparking device to ignite it."

"The setup was a cinch," Frank added. "Anyone

going down there was bound to follow the car's trail through the bush – and the trip wire would never be seen in the dark."

Collig nodded grimly. "The timer was evidently set to allow just enough delay for you boys to get close to the station wagon after tripping the wire. Really a fiendish setup!"

"It gets rid of the car, too," Frank pointed out, "with no risk of fingerprints or other clues being left behind."

A twisted, blackened shell was all that remained after the flames died out. Any traces of the timing mechanism had been fused and obliterated by the intense heat. Somewhat shaken by the experience, Frank and Joe drove home.

Mr Hardy frowned worriedly upon hearing of their narrow escape. "This proves you're up against highly dangerous criminals, sons."

"More than petty thieves," Frank agreed.

"Definitely – which points back to the industrial spy ring again. From now on, I want you both to be on your guard at all times."

"We will, Dad," Joe promised. He told of their hunch about Soapy Moran's visit.

"Soapy Moran, eh?" Mr Hardy strode to his criminal file, leafed through a number of photographs, and finally pulled out a pair of mug shots. "Is that the man?"

Both boys recognized the swindler at once.

"He has a record as a small-time con man and pickpocket," Mr Hardy told them. "Offhand, I wouldn't think he's the type to be mixed up in anything bigger – but I'll ask the FBI to put out a dragnet for him, just in case."

The evening was too far spent to allow much time for work on the code message. All three Hardys puzzled over it for a while, but finally went to bed with no glimmer of a solution.

The next day Mike and Tommy arrived promptly after school, eager for a taxidermy lesson. "Jimmy said he had a lot of work to do for his ma," Mike explained.

Later, Frank and Joe found the two youngsters watching with close attention as Chet smoothed out a paper head form.

"It's made to the exact measurement of the deer's head," Chet was saying. "When the skin comes back from the tanner's, we shall apply that over the form. Then Professor Morton will demonstrate how much better this is than the older stuffing methods. It's all a matter of expert judgement and know-how, of course." Chet cleared his throat importantly.

The Hardys suppressed grins. "Don't let us interrupt, Professor," Frank said.

"Matter of fact, I was about to break off for an errand," the stout youth announced. "Have to pick up a couple of glass eyes in town."

Joe glanced around the cluttered work space. Scrap lumber, cotton batting, galvanized wire, and an old oil-paint set lay strewn about the floor. Along with books and tools on the bench were a partly mounted duck and rabbit supplied by hunter friends, a pasty substance, and lumps of unfired clay. Various chemical bottles were lined up on a shelf behind Chet.

"Boy, this looks like a warehouse for a mad scientist," Joe remarked. "You *are* going to clean up in here some time, aren't you?"

"Natch. What do you think I have a staff for?" Wiping borax-covered hands on his apron, Chet added, "Mike, I hereby appoint you vice-president in charge of cleanup. Tommy, you finish sanding the wood base for this duck. And when you're done" — Chet pulled a sack of fudge out of a bench drawer and popped a piece into his mouth — 'help yourself to some of this yummy confection. Made it myself!"

As the youngsters set about their tasks eagerly, Joe shot an amused glance at Frank. "What an operator! Maybe we Hardys should get a cooking staff in case Aunt Gertrude goes visiting and doesn't leave any pie, cake, or cookies for Chet."

The stout boy grimaced.

Frank grinned and declined Chet's invitation to help pick out glass eyes for his deer, preferring to work on the code message. Joe, however, was willing to go. He and Chet strode out to the Queen and soon the yellow jalopy was clattering noisily towards downtown Bayport.

Roundtree's Taxidermy Shop was as dark as a cave and twice as mysterious. From the shadows of its dim interior, white fangs and sharp claws gleamed menacingly at the two boys. Near the door, a huge grizzly bear reared on its hind legs as if ready to pounce on any customer who caused its master displeasure.

Mr Roundtree, a short, plump man, shuffled about in flapping slippers. As the boys entered, he was completing the sale of a mounted wolf's head to a man in a tan raincoat and slouch hat. Joe glanced curiously at the animal, then turned with Chet to a display case of glass eyes.

"Don't you want me to crate it?" Joe heard Mr Roundtree ask the customer.

"Don't bother!" The man snatched the wolf's head off the counter and turned to leave.

"Er – you haven't paid me, sir."

"What? . . . Oh, sorry." As the man stopped to fumble for his wallet, Joe glanced at him. In spite of the low slouch hat shadowing his face, Joe felt that the man looked familiar.

Their eyes met for a moment. Without another word he stuffed the wallet back into his pocket and darted towards the door!

"My money, sir!" Mr Roundtree exclaimed. But the customer was already out of the shop – the door slamming shut behind him.

Suddenly Joe's memory clicked. No wonder he had not recognized the fellow with the hat on!

"Chet! That was the baldheaded thief at the auction!" he cried, dashing from the store.

Chet stared open-mouthed, then trotted after Joe as Roundtree gaped in helpless bewilderment. The thief was nowhere in sight, yet he could not have taken a car – there was a solid line of automobiles parked at the curb.

"Wh-which way did he go?" Chet demanded.

"Don't ask me!" Joe ran to a girl who was standing in front of a florist's window. "Did you see a man with a wolf's head just now?"

"A man with a *wolf's* head?" The girl looked at Joe suspiciously. "Are you kidding?"

Joe reddened and started to explain, then gave up. "Oh, never mind – thanks just the same!"

He ran up the street, then down, with Chet at his heels, looking in stores and questioning passersby. None had seen the man. Discouraged, the boys started back to the taxidermy shop.

"I can't understand it," Joe said. "That man came out of the store only a few minutes ago. He couldn't vanish into thin air."

Just then a woman's shrill scream brought the boys to a halt. Joe and Chet exchanged startled glances. Another scream split the air.

"In there!" Joe pointed to Zetter's Radio and TV Store, next to Roundtree's. The two youths dashed inside. There were no customers in sight, nor anyone at the counter.

From somewhere in back, they heard a door burst open and a loud, frightened sob. Guided by the sound, Joe and Chet darted into a narrow passageway leading to the rear of the shop.

A woman stumbled into view, pale with fright. "Th-there's a wild animal out there!" She pointed to the back door. "Something ferocious! I was taking a shortcut through the alley when I saw it! It scared the wits out of me!"

By this time a policeman and several other people were crowding into the store. Joe and Chet ran out the back door into the alley.

"She's nutty!" Chet declared, looking all around. "There's no animal out here!"

Then Joe caught a glimpse of baleful eyes and gleaming fangs. "Oh, yes, there is!"

With a chuckle, he pointed down the steps of a depressed cellar entrance to their right. Propped near the cellar door in the shadowy gloom was the mounted wolf's head, looking as if the whole animal were about to come bounding out of the darkness!

"Good grief!" said Chet. "So that's what scared her. I guess this explains how that crook got away, too."

"Sure. He was afraid I might remember his face, so he ran through Zetter's right after he left Roundtree's – and dumped the wolf here so no one would spot him making his getaway."

As Joe retrieved the wolf's head, Mr Zetter, a tall, dark-featured man, came up the alley. He frowned at the noisy hubbub outside his shop.

"What's going on here?" he snapped. As the boys explained, Zetter snorted irritably. "A fine how-d'you-do! I leave the store for a few minutes to get a sandwich and find the place in an uproar when I get back!"

He strode inside, the boys following. The woman gave another gasp of alarm when she saw the wolf's head in Joe's arms. She soon calmed down, however, and smiled shamefacedly upon realizing her mistake. After Joe had reported the auction thief's getaway to the policeman, the two boys returned the head to Roundtree's and Chet purchased glass eyes for his deer.

By the time they arrived at the Hardy house on Elm Street, Fenton Hardy was home. He listened with a wry grin of amusement to Joe's story. "Good work, son, recognizing that bald auction thief. But what about the wolf's head?"

"We took it back to the taxidermy shop." Joe paused as he saw his father frown slightly. "Was that a wrong move?"

"Well, it might have been wiser to leave it where you found it. If the thief stashed the head there, he may have been planning to come back for it later. In your place, I would have staked out the alley and kept watch."

"I should've thought of that!" Joe chided himself.

"Maybe it's not too late," Frank spoke up. "Come on. Joe. Let's give it a try!"

Leaving Chet at work with the youngsters, the Hardys drove downtown. At the taxidermy shop they received bad news.

"Sorry boys," Mr Roundtree reported. "That fellow came back and snatched the wolf's head right off the counter. He was out of the store before I had time to blink."

Joe groaned. "Did he go off in a car?"

"'Fraid I didn't notice. To tell the truth, I hardly had time to collect my wits."

"Say," Frank asked on a sudden hunch, "do you happen to know who mounted that wolf's head?"

"Why yes. It was an old customer of mine – Elias Batter."

·8·

A Secret Treasure

Elias Batter – the late owner of the stuffed animals stolen at the auction! And now another of his mounted specimens had been purchased by one of the thieves! Mr Roundtree peered shrewdly at the Hardys as he saw their startled looks.

"Did you boys know Mr Batter?" the taxidermist asked.

"Not personally," Frank replied, "but we've heard of him. You say he was a customer?"

"Roundtree nodded. "Used to drop in often for supplies. Can't say I cared for him much."

"Why not?" Joe queried.

"Oh, I don't know. Struck me as a sly, disagreeable sort." The taxidermist gave a slight, embarrassed cough. "Maybe I shouldn't be saying that."

"How'd you happen to get the wolf's head?" Frank queried.

Roundtree explained that Batter had traded it to him for several unprepared pelts. "Good trade, too. Elias Batter was a fine craftsman – his work would stand out anywhere. And – "

"You mean you could actually identify animals that he stuffed?" Joe put in.

"Yep." Roundtree described thick eye-waxing,

dramatic poses, and meticulous double sewing as characteristics of Batter's craftmanship. "Particularly the sewing. He had a way of using extra stitches on a skin."

Glancing at Frank, Joe could see that his brother had been struck by the same idea. This might explain how the thief had spotted the wolf as Batter's work!

"Did you have the wolf's head displayed in the window?" Frank asked.

"Yes. The man you're looking for came in and asked for it specially."

"How long ago was it that he came back?"

"Not long. You didn't miss him by more than two minutes."

Disgusted at their bad luck, the Hardys thanked Mr Roundtree and left his shop. A freckle-faced boy was lounging against their convertible. "Well, what d'you know? It's our little pal!" Joe exclaimed. "Hi, Jimmy!"

"Hi." The youngster acknowledged their greeting rather glumly. "I saw you two go in there, so I thought I'd wait. Just wanted to explain why I didn't show up today."

"That's all right," Frank said. "Mike told us you had to do some things for your mother."

"Uh-huh. She came home early and made me do a lot of work." Jimmy reached into the convertible and pulled out a bag of groceries which he had set on the back seat. "Like going to the store for this stuff."

"Put it back," Frank advised. "We'll give you a lift home."

Jimmy brightened at the prospect of another ride in

the convertible with the top down. As the car swung away from the curb, Joe queried, "You said you saw us go into the taxidermist's?"

"Yeah, I was standing in front of Zetter's window, watching a colour TV," Jimmy replied.

"You didn't happen to notice a man come out of Roundtree's carrying a wolf's head?"

"Sure, he was parked in front – right where you guys parked."

"What kind of car?" Frank asked eagerly.

"A green four-door."

"The same one he and his partner were driving on Sunday, I'll bet!" Joe exclaimed.

Jimmy looked from one Hardy boy to the other. "What's the deal? Is he some kind of a crook?"

"Sure is! He's one of the auction thieves." Joe immediately warmed up the convertible's shortwave and reported this latest development to the police.

At the tenement house where the Gordons lived, Frank suggested that he and Joe go in and meet Jimmy's mother. He agreed, but without enthusiasm.

Frank and Joe accomapanied him up two flights of rickety stairs, then along a corridor with paint-peeling walls. Jimmy opened the door to the Gordon's apartment and led them inside.

A woman peered from the kitchen, which gave off an aroma of boiling cabbage. Seeing the Hardys, she came out, wiping her hands on her apron. She would have been attractive looking except for the lines of care in her face.

"Ma, this is Frank and Joe Hardy, the guys I was telling you about," Jimmy mumbled.

"Oh, yes." The detective's sons, aren't you? Pleased to meet you." Shaking hands, she gave the Hardys a rather suspicious stare. "Real big-hearted of you, taking Jimmy home to dinner last night. Saved me cooking for him."

"We enjoyed having him," Frank said.

Mrs Gordon's lips formed a grudging smile. "Hope he behaved himself." Her smile faded as she added, "Can't stay out of mischief, most of the time, and he won't pay attention at school, either. Needs a father's hand – that's the whole trouble."

"He'll shape up. Won't you, Jimmy?" Joe said, rumpling the youngster's hair.

There was a moment's awkward silence.

"Jimmy says Elias Batter was his uncle," Frank ventured cautiously.

"Oh, he does, does he?" Mrs Gordon frowned and Jimmy moved off sullenly, pretending to toy with a coloured paperweight on a table.

"Did you ever hear Mr Batter speak of a man named Soapy Moran?" Joe asked.

"No, I didn't!" Mrs Gordon snapped, her face hardening. "I got better things to do than poke my nose into Eli's affairs! And what's more, they're none of your business, either!"

The Hardys reddened at the unexpected outburst, Joe tried to explain the reason for his query, but Mrs Gordon brusquely cut him off.

"I – er – guess we'd better be going," Frank said. "Nice to have met you, Mrs Batter."

As they retreated down the hall, Joe gulped. "Whew! I sure pulled a boner that time."

"Guess we both did," Frank said. "I probably shouldn't have brought up Batter's name. Remember, Jimmy told us his mother wouldn't have anything to do with his uncle Elly.'

That evening Mr Hardy was called away for an urgent meeting with a client on an insurance investigation. After studying for a couple of hours, Frank and Joe worked the ham bands for a while in their attic shack. Then they turned their attention once more to the uncracked code message.

"It's a cinch this can't be a simple substitution or transposition cipher," Joe mused.

"Not with this mixture of words and numbers," Frank agreed. "What puzzles me is the – "

He broke off as Aunt Gertrude called up, "There's a visitor here to see you two!"

Frank and Joe hurried downstairs. Jimmy Gordon was waiting in the living room. The freckle-faced youngster looked embarrassed as they greeted him.

"How about some cocoa and cookies?" Frank suggested. Jimmy seemed to relax as they enjoyed their snack in the kitchen. But not until they went up to the radio shack and let him listen in on a call from a ham in Texas did he speak of the reason for his visit.

"Sorry Ma got so sore at you fellows this afternoon," Jimmy mumbled awkwardly. "I figured I ought to sneak over and explain."

"*Sneak* over?" Joe said. "Won't she worry?"

"Aw, she's out gabbing with one of the neighbours. Besides, she was picking on me all through supper, so she'll know why I didn't stick around." Jimmy paused and then went on, "You see, Ma always gets worked up when anyone mentions Uncle Elly. She says he was a crook and made trouble for the whole family."

"I'm sorry, Jimmy," Frank apologized. "We didn't realize that."

"Aw, it's not your fault."

"Why did she consider your uncle a crook?" Joe asked, after exchanging glances with Frank. "Had he ever been convicted of breaking the law?"

"No, not that I know of," Jimmy replied. "But he was Ma's oldest brother, and she says he was always getting into some kind of scrapes. Once he almost got sent up for robbing the Crescent Jewellery Store."

"Oh, when was that?" Frank inquired.

"Oh, when I was little. I don't remember much about it, but Uncle Elly was living with us then. That was before he got married. The police came around and questioned everybody at our place, even Ma and Dad."

"Sounds pretty unpleasant," Joe remarked sympathetically.

"Ma sure thought so." Jimmy's face took on a resentful scowl. "We were living in a better neighbourhood then, and she says no one on the block would have anything to do with us after that. Dad even lost his job at the bank on account of it."

Frank said, "And your mother blamed your uncle Elly?"

"Uh-huh. The cops never did prove he was guilty, but she made him move out of the house."

"But you still went on seeing him?"

Jimmy shrugged. "He'd drop in sometimes when

she wasn't home. And after Dad died, he used to slip me money."

The youngster fidgeted silently for a moment. Frank and Joe said nothing, sensing that he was on the verge of revealing something more.

"Look, can you guys keep a secret?"

"Of course we can," Frank assured him. "What's on your mind?"

"Uncle Elly had something hidden away for me. Something valuable. That's what I was looking for the other night."

"What is it?" Joe asked.

Jimmy shrugged. "He wouldn't tell me. It was like this. I went to visit him once after he got sick. He said, "Jimmy boy, if anything happens to me, I got something secret hidden away that could be worth plenty!"

"He didn't tell you *where* it was hidden?" Frank queried.

"Nope. When I asked him, he just laughed and said, 'Look in the right spots and you'll find it.' Then he had a fit of coughing. When he got his breath back, he said, 'I'll tell you later, when the time comes.' But it turned out that was the last time I ever saw him."

The Hardys frowned thoughtfully, turning the problem over in their minds.

Jimmy asked earnestly, "Will you guys help me find it? If it *is* worth a lot, like Uncle Elly said, Ma could sure use the dough."

"You bet we'll help you," Frank promised, patting the boy's shoulder. "As a matter of fact, we expect to go over to your uncle's house soon. Maybe we can look around then."

Jimmy left, looking happier than the Hardys had yet seen him. Joe took him to the front door. When he returned to the attic, he found Frank twirling the tuning dial absently, his thoughts obviously far from the ham bands.

"What do you make of that story Jimmy told us?" Joe broke in.

"It could explain a lot," Frank replied. "If Batter hid something valuable, that might even be what the auction thieves were after."

"Suppose we were lucky enough to find it," Joe said. "How could we prove Batter meant it for Jimmy? Wouldn't it be Mrs Batter's property?"

Frank's face grew troubled. "Good question, I'm not sure if – "

He broke off with a startled look as a voice suddenly blurted from the speaker:

"*Aardvark bulldog . . . Aardvark bulldog . . .*"

"The code voice again!" Frank gasped, hastily adjusting the tuning.

A moment later came the sound of barking. Frank snatched pencil and paper and wrote down the message that followed:

> 24 1 ARRESTED LEK 4 2 REVEALED
> 9 5 STATED 97 3 OVERHAUL.

The Tabloid Key

The Hardys listened breathlessly as the message was repeated. Once more came a series of loud barks. Then the sounds faded.

"What a break!" Joe exclaimed.

"It's not over the same frequency," Frank noted, "but pretty close. They probably vary their transmitting frequency on a regular schedule."

Joe nodded as he pulled up a chair. "We were lucky to pick 'em up twice!" Eagerly the two boys settled down to compare the new message with the one they had received earlier.

"They're both in the same code," Frank remarked. "That's obvious just from looking at them. What beats me is the way the numbers alternate with words."

"Me, too," Joe agreed in a puzzled voice. "Either one by itself might indicate a fairly simple cipher. Or they might refer to a codebook. But the two mixed together . . ." he shook his head, mystified.

"You may have something there, though," Frank said. "The numbers are given in pairs, just as they would be for a dictionary code. One might be the page number, and the other the number of the word on the page."

"In that case, why give any words at all?"

"That doesn't make sense to me, either." Frank brooded silently for a few moments, then said, "Another thing. You'll notice that some words are preceded by a pair of numbers and some aren't."

"Right," Joe responded. "In the first message, for instance, there are no numbers before 'sheep' or 'hairs,' and in the second message – "

"Hold it! Say those words again!"

Joe obliged. "Sheep. Hairs. What about them?"

"Don't you get it?" Frank said. "The 'aardvark bulldog' bit indicates the gang may be using animal code names – "

Joe nodded. "Sure. Aardvark calling Bulldog. And the barking is Bulldog's response, meaning 'I read you.' So what?"

"So 'sheep' and 'hairs' may be animal names, too – for other members of the gang. Not h-a-i-r-s but *h-a-r-e-s*. I just wrote it down wrong."

"Wow!" Joe's eyes lit up excitedly. "I'll bet you're right. And that may explain why 'sheep' and 'hares' have no numbers in front of them. Bulldog already knows those names, so he doesn't need any codebook numbers to look up their meaning."

"Whoa! You're jumping way ahead of me," Frank said, "but I think we're on the same track. You're implying that the other words *do* have to be looked up."

"Sure. Maybe not in a regular codebook, but some other book they're using as a key. Bulldog uses the numbers to locate each message-word in the key. Then he decodes by taking the first word that follows each of the message-words – or maybe the second word, or the word just before each message-word."

Joe paused and frowned. "What about 'lek,' though? No numbers in front of that, but I never heard of any animal called a lek."

Frank grinned. "Neither did I, but it could still be a code name that Bulldog already knows. Getting back to this code-key book, what do you suppose they might be using?"

"Boy! Ask me something easy!" Joe grumbled. "It might be *any* book – any one they'd agreed on beforehand."

"Wait a seond. Maybe the numbers don't refer to a book at all," Frank said.

"Why not?"

"If they *were* using a book, they'd only need a single number, not a pair of numbers," Frank argued. "For instance, take the opening of the first message '7 2 progress.' You might turn to page seven, find the word *progress* on that page, and then translate by taking the next word that follows. Where would the '2' come in?"

"Simple," said Joe. "Take the second word after progress."

Frank stared at his brother. "You know, that may be the answer! But it sure leaves us up a tree. Without knowing the book, we can't possibly hope to crack the code."

For more than an hour, the young sleuths continued to pore over the messages, but neither could think of any other possible solution. Fenton Hardy had not returned home when they finally gave up and prepared for bed. Joe had switched off the light and settled back on his pillow when Frank exclaimed, 'Hey! We're prize dopes!"

"How come?" Joe demanded sleepily.

"The code name could be a newspaper – not a book! The two numbers could stand for the page *and column!*'

Joe was instantly wide awake. Switching on their bedside light again, the boys consulted the two code messages, which they had brought down from the attic.

"Look! This bears me out!" Frank said. "The second number is always small, just as it would be if it stood for a column."

"Now all we have to do is figure out which paper," Joe sid wryly.

"I'd say a New York paper's the best bet," Frank conjectured. "They're the most widely circulated in this part of the country."

"Hmm. Let's see,' Joe mused. "One of the numbers in the second message is 97. If that's a page number, it would have to be a pretty thick newspaper."

"Right." Frank scowled intently, then snapped his fingers. "None of the column numbers is higher than 5 – which sounds like a tabloid. Full-sized newspapers run to eight or nine columns. And tabloids are often pretty thick, too. I'm sure the *Star* runs to about a hundred pages."

"Man, oh man! Let's whip down to the station first thing tomorrow and see if we can still get a copy of today's *Star!*"

Next morning when the boys came down to breakfast, they learned that their father had already left the house – this time for another flying trip to New York. Disappointed at missing him, Frank and Joe ate their bacon and eggs, then drove to the Bayport railroad station.

"Got a Wednesday *Star* left?" Frank asked the newsdealer.

"Sure." The man reached down behind the counter and brought up a copy. Frank paid for it and hurried back to their car.

"Let's check out the first word in the message," Joe said eagerly. "Page twenty-four, column one – 'arrested.'"

Frank leafed to the right page and ran his finger down the first column. Almost at once he came to a sentence using the word *arrested*:

Three suspected smugglers were arrested in a raid on a Lower East Side warehouse early this morning.

"Wow! How do you like that?" Joe exulted.

Frank glanced at his wristwatch. "Sufferin' snakes! We're almost late for class!"

With a roar of exhaust, the convertible headed for Bayport High School. Not until they returned home that afternoon were the Hardys able to resume work on the code message.

"Did you look up the other words?" Frank asked as Joe spread the *Star* on the dining-room table.

"I sure did – and they all check out." Joe leafed

through the paper and pointed to three more sentences which he had circled in pencil:

In a news conference today, the NASA flight director **revealed** *that a plant was being built in Wyoming to assemble the new rocket booster.*

Commissioner Mason **stated** *that the new freight rates would go into effect immediately.*

"We plan to **overhaul** *our whole setup," Barnes announced at yesterday's stockholders' meeting.*

"So far so good!" Frank said with a cautious grin. "Now let's see what we can make of the whole message. Try writing down the first word that follows each of the code words."

"Okay." Joe picked them out of the newspaper sentences and jotted them down, including 'lek' in its proper position. The result read:

IN LEK THAT THAT OUR.

Joe snorted in disgust. "It doesn't make sense."

"Let's try the second word after each code word." This time the result read:

A LEK A THE WHOLE.

"Still no sense," Joe commented. "Let's try the third words."

Just then, Chet Morton's jalopy pulled into the drive and he shouted "Hello" to the Hardys. Frank went to the back door to answer his greeting and invited the stout youth inside. The two boys found Joe looking excited as they entered the dining room.

"Take a look at this, Frank! I think we've got something this time!" Joe pointed to the latest result which he had written down:

RAID LEK PLANT NEW SETUP.

"What gives?" Chet inquired. "You guys working on another mystery or something?"

"We're trying to crack a code message." As Frank explained, Chet's eyes took on a sudden gleam of interest.

"Lex plant . . . Hey! That could mean the Lextrex plant where Biff Hooper's working!" he exclaimed.

Biff Hooper, a high school chum, had recently taken a weekend job as watchman at an electronics company. Its factory was located near Willow River outside Bayport. Joe and Frank looked at Chet in astonishment.

"Morton, you're a genius!" Joe said. "Lextrex just added a new addition, didn't it, Frank?"

"That's right – which would explain the 'new setup' part of the message!"

The Hardy boys were impatient to report their discovery to their father. When he arrived home that evening, Mr Hardy listened keenly as Frank and Joe told how they had decoded the message.

"Hmm. That's pretty convincing," the detective said. "It certainly seems more than a coincidence that you found each of the message-words in the correct pages and columns. But are you sure this is the only possible translation?"

"We've tried other arrangements, Dad, just to double-check," Frank said. "For instance, we tried taking words that come *before* the code words. But this is the only version that makes any sense."

Mr Hardy paced about the room. "'Raid' sounds as if they're planning a robbery," he mused. "But the industrial spy gang has never done that. They seem to have gleaned their trade secrets by inside leaks."

"Maybe that's what this message means, Dad," Joe suggested. "It could be an order to some inside man at Lektrex to snitch data about what's going on in the new plant wing."

The detective nodded slowly. "Yes, that may be it. I'd better get in touch with Jason Warner right away. He's the president."

Mr Hardy telephoned and managed to reach the company official at his home. When he hung up, the detective told Frank and Joe, "Warner didn't seem much alarmed. He'll see us at four o'clock tomorrow afternoon."

The next day the Hardy boys drove from school to the Lektrex plant. They met their father in the lobby. A secretary ushered them into a conference room adjoining the president's office.

Jason Warner, brisk and grey-haired, shook hands with the Hardys and invited them to sit down. "Good of you to take so much trouble on our account," he said. "I'd like to hear more about this spy threat."

Frank and Joe explained the code message. Mr Hardy gave a brief rundown on the other industrial espionage cases he had investigated.

Warner smiled and said sceptically, "This whole

thing sounds pretty far-fetched to me. We've never had any trouble at Lektrex."

"Exactly what *is* going on in your new plant wing?" Fenton Hardy inquired.

"We're producing a new type of thin-film circuitry," Warner replied. "It's fairly confidential, but the same electronics engineers who design our other products are working on it."

"They've all undergone security checks?"

"Absolutely! I'm confident none of them would do anything underhanded." The Lektrex president frowned and drummed his fingers on the conference table. "However, to make absolutely certain, I'd like to engage you to double-check the clearance on all our key personnel."

"Very well," Mr Hardy agreed.

Frank had noticed a stuffed fox, mounted on a shelf, attached to one wall of the conference room. He gave Joe a nudge and pointed it out. While Mr Warner called his secretary and asked her to send for the personnel manager, the two boys got up from the table to examine the animal.

The fox was crouched in a dramatic, lifelike pose, fangs bared as if about to spring on its prey. Frank's eyes suddenly widened. "Joe," he whispered, "look at this double-stitching!"

"Oh, oh!" Joe's face reflected his brother's excitement. "Just the way Mr Roundtree described Batter's work!"

Was the fox another of Elias Batter's mysterious stuffed specimens?

10

Mysterious Cries

"Mr Warner, where did this stuffed fox come from?" Frank asked.

The company president looked up absently. From a friend of mine in New York who's in the decorating business. Quite a striking specimen, isn't it?"

"Yes, it is," Frank said. "We thought it might be the work of a taxidermist we know of – a man named Elias Batter."

The Hardy boys waited expectantly to see if Batter's name would evoke any response. Warner merely shook his head. "I never heard of him."

An hour later, after reviewing the files on various key people at the plant with Jason Warner and his personnel manager, the detective stood up to leave. "This may have been a false alarm," he told them, "But it won't hurt to make sure."

Mr Hardy, who had come to Lektrex in a taxi, walked out with Frank and Joe to their convertible on the plant parking lot. On the way home Joe said, "It'll take a while to run checks on all those people, won't it?"

His father nodded. "I'll put Sam Radley and some of my other operatives on it right away. We'll cross-check all names with the FBI, too." He turned to

Frank at the wheel. "I'm wondering why you asked Mr Warner about the fox."

"It just seemed like an odd coincidence if it *was* Batter's work. But I guess we were wrong."

"That reminds me, Dad," Joe put in, "do you recall a robbery a few years ago at the Crescent Jewellery Store?" He related what Jimmy Gordon had said about the suspicion against his uncle.

"Hmm. It comes back to me vaguely," Mr Hardy replied. "A valuable diamond necklace was taken – a necklace with perfectly matched pearshaped stones. The case was never solved."

Joe gave a low, excited whistle and Fenton Hardy narrowed his eyes shrewdly. "You think the necklace may have something to do with those animals that were stolen from the auction?"

"It's a possibility, Dad," Frank spoke up. "If the crooks thought Batter still had the stones, they might figure one of his stuffed animals would be a likely hiding place."

Joe added, "They might even *know* he had the stones – especially if they were on the robbery with him. What's more, Batter told Jimmy that he had something secret hidden away, something that was 'worth plenty,' and he wanted Jimmy to have it if anything happened to him."

"Hidden in the house?" Mr Hardy asked.

"I guess so, but Jimmy doesn't know. His uncle apparently intended to tell him, but they never saw each other again before Batter died."

Reaching Elm Street, Frank garaged the car and

they went into the house. Aunt Gertrude was testing a roast chicken in the oven.

"Humph! About time you three were getting home!" she said severely. "I was beginning to think this bird might go to waste."

"No danger." Fenton Hardy grinned. "If the boys aren't hungry, I'll eat it all myself."

"Who said we aren't hungry?" Joe retorted, sniffing the delicious aroma. "Mmm! Aunt Gertrude, you sure know how to cook poultry."

"Never mind buttering me up," she said. "You boys had a phone call, by the way."

"From whom, Aunty?" Frank inquired.

"That lawyer, J. Sylvester Crowell. Said he'd be in his office till six, and if he didn't hear from you, he might call back this evening."

Joe snapped his fingers eagerly. "Maybe he's been in touch with Mrs Batter!"

"There's still time to reach him," Frank said, glancing at the clock. "Let's try."

The boys hurried to the telephone and Frank dialled the attorney. Crowell himself answered.

"I called in regard to your request to visit the Batter house," he told Frank.

"You've spoken to Mrs Batter about it?"

"Yes. She thinks it very unlikely that you can gain any clues from the remaining stuffed animals. However, she's willing to have you take a look at them – on condition that you don't disturb anything else in the house."

"Of course not," Frank promised. "When could we go over?"

"It would have to be tonight, I'm afraid. Mrs Batter is only in town for one day, and she's leaving again in the morning to visit her sister." Crowell added that the boys would have to pick up the key at Mrs Batter's apartment, and gave her address.

"Right, sir," Frank said, jotting it down. "We'll stop there about a quarter to eight."

Mrs Batter received the boys with a cold, beady-eyed stare. "Just what is it you expect to find?" she demanded.

Frank smiled and shrugged. "Maybe nothing. But if there's anything special about the stuffed animals your husband made, the ones still at the house may give us a clue."

"What do you mean by 'anything special'?"

"If we knew the answer to that," Joe said, "we'd probably have this case solved."

"You certainly don't seem to be making much progress," the widow snapped. "However, if you think it'll do any good, go ahead and look. The electricity is still on. But I shall expect to have the key back tonight. Is that clear?"

"Yes, Mrs Batter," Frank said.

As the boys drove away, Joe grumbled, "You'd think she was doing us a favour!"

Frank chuckled. "Maybe she is, if this trip helps us turn up any clues to Jimmy's treasure."

The temperature had dropped sharply since sunset, and the boys drove with their convertible top raised and the heater on. Joe noticed his brother watching the rear-view mirror. "What's the matter? Someone on our tail?"

"I thought so for a while," Frank said. "Guess I was mistaken, though."

On Hill Road they turned up the gravel driveway to the Batter house and climbed out of their car. The boys mounted the porch and Frank inserted the key in the front-door lock. The door creaked open. Both Hardys switched on flashlights and probed the darkness until Joe located a huge, draughty hallway with a winding staircase at the far end.

"Let's take a look upstairs first," Frank suggested.

"Okay." The boys could see their breath in the chilly atmosphere. The wind outside echoed through the house and rattled the shutters.

On the second floor the young sleuths moved from room to room, playing their flashlight beams into each one. All seemed bare and empty except for worn carpeting and a few items of old furniture.

"It would sure take more than one evening to tap for hollow walls and check the flooring in a house this size," Joe murmured.

Frank nodded gloomily. "We'll just have to keep our eyes open for anything unusual."

One room with a workbench and a musty odour appeared to have been Batter's taxidermy shop. A scarred desk stood in one corner. Joe pulled open the drawers. They seemed to contain only odds and ends, such as old receipted bills.

"Let's go through these papers before we leave," Frank said, "to be sure we don't miss anything."

The attic and downstairs rooms were also largely empty. At the rear, the boys discovered what might have been intended originally as a games room.

Mounted heads of a deer, a moose, a rhinoerous, and a Canada lynx glared eerily from the walls.

On the dusty fireplace mantel were a stuffed owl and a snake. Joe picked up the latter. On its wooden base was a metal plate which read:

SPECKLED KING SNAKE
MOUNTED BY D. CARSON

"D. Carson," Joe muttered. "Who's he?"

"Some pal of Batter's, I suppose," frank said.

The owl and rhinocerous had similar plates. Seeing none on the deer, Frank lifted it down from the wall. "This must be Batter's work. Let's see if we can find anything unusual about it."

The boys examined the head carefully. Several fine puncture marks were clearly visible around the muzzle and eyes. As Joe fingered the fine hairs, he discovered other holes. "Looks as if someone's been probing it with a hatpin."

"Probably Mrs Batter!" Frank exclaimed. "She must suspect the same thing we do – that her husband hid something in one of the – "

A weird shriek from outside startled the boys.

"Good night!" said Joe. "That wasn't the wind, was it?"

As if in answer came another wailing cry, then another.

"Those are human voices!" Frank exclaimed. "Out in the back somewhere!"

It was impossible to see anything from the windows. The boys dashed into the hallway, then through the kitchen to the back door. As they stepped on to the open rear porch, both aimed their flashlights beams into the darkness.

Joe started to say, "Do you hear anyth – " But his voice choked off as something struck him a hard blow on the back of the head!

Frank turned and saw his brother crumple. Then he, too, was struck down from behind!

·11·

Night Alarm

When Frank opened his eyes, he was still lying on the porch. His head throbbed and he was chilled to the bone. Suddenly he saw his brother's still figure. Frank raised himself.

"Joe! Joe, are you all right?"

The only response was a faint moan, but after Frank had shaken him, his brother's eyes opened. "L-l-leapin' lizards! What happened?"

"Someone conked us. Can you stand up?"

"Sure, I guess so." Stiffly the boys struggled to their feet. Joe shook his head. "Whew! We sure walked into a trap!"

"You can say that again," Frank agreed wryly. "Those spooky wails we heard were just a trick to get us out here. The guys who beaned us must have been waiting right outside the door."

Joe cast an anxious glance towards the lighted windows. "What do you suppose they were after?"

"Don't know. But I could sure make a guess!"

Impelled by the same thought, the boys re-entered the house cautiously. No one was in sight and there was not a sound. As they came into the games room, Joe gave a gasp of dismay.

"The stuffed animals are gone!"

"Not all of them," Frank said. The rhinoceros head, owl, and snake had not been taken.

Joe surveyed the remaining specimens with a look of gloomy satisfaction. "Well, at least this proves our theory. They took only the animals Batter himself had stuffed, so they're definitely looking for something he stashed inside one of them."

Frank nodded. "We'd better notify the police."

"I'll call them on our short-wave." Joe hurried out to the boys' convertible. The police operator promised to send a prowl car.

When Joe returned to the house, his brother was coming down the staircase. "The animals were't all they took," Frank said.

"What else?"

"They rifled Batter's desk and stole all the papers from the drawers."

"I don't get it," Joe said, puzzled. "If they were after something hidden in the animals, why bother with papers?"

Frank shook his head, equally mystified. "I don't get it, either."

The police car soon arrived. Two officers took down the boys' story and made a brief search, but found no traces left by the thieves. "You fellows feel well enough to go home alone?" one officer asked.

"Sure, we're okay," Frank said. "Just a couple of lumps on our heads."

"Let's hope we don't wind up with any more when we tell Mrs Batter what happened," Joe said ruefully. "We have to return her key."

The widow seemed less upset by the news than the

Hardys had feared. "I doubt that what the sneaks got will be worth much," she scoffed.

"Maybe their first haul, from the auction wasn't worth much, either," Frank said, "and that's why they came back for a second try."

Mrs Batter's green eyes narrowed. She started to say something, then seemed to check himself. "Humph! Well, don't expect me to pay any medical bills!" she snapped. "What happened was your own fault."

As the Hardy's left in their convertible, Joe said, "I'll bet she did that probing with a hatpin, all right. That's why she didn't get much worked up about this theft."

Frank grinned drily. "She's satisfied there was nothing in the heads – but she still doesn't want to talk about it."

They were just pulling up their driveway when Frank slammed on the brakes. The beam from their headlights showed Chet's stuffed aardvark lying in front of the garage!

"What's that doing out here?" Joe exclaimed. Both boys jumped from the car. The kitchen was ablaze with light. Sensing something wrong, Frank and Joe dashed inside.

Aunt Gertrude was seated at the table, sipping tea. "Well!" She snifed. "Too bad you weren't here five minutes ago when I needed you."

"What happened, Aunty?" Frank demanded.

Miss Hardy explained that their father had gone to see Sam Radley, his chief operative. She herself had dozed off in front of the TV set. Suddenly she had been awakened by a noise at the back of the house. When she went to investigate, she had glimpsed a prowler in the garage.

"Wow! What did you do?" Joe asked.

"What *could* I do – a weak woman with no menfolk in the house to protect me!" Miss Hardy glared at the boys over her teacup. "I took a broom to him, naturally."

Frank and Joe burst out laughing.

"I'm sorry, Aunt Gertrude," Frank said, choking, "but I wish we could have seen that!"

"He must have been trying to get away with the aardvark," Joe declared.

"He was, but he dropped it fast when I swatted him," Miss Hardy said tartly. "Then I was so overcome with shock, I had to come in and make myself some tea." She added after another sip, "He must have had a car. I heard it speed off."

Frank snapped his fingers. "We'd better look and see if he got the bear!"

The two boys hurried out to the garage. Nothing but the aardvark had been disturbed.

"He may have been hoping to get both animals, though," Joe said. "You know, Frank, we're a couple of champs. We never even thought of investigating Chet's stuffed specimens!"

"You're telling me. I wonder if we can get him to rip them apart so we can take a look."

"We'd better," Joe said. "If none of the other animals contained anything, the bear or the aardvark might hold the answer!"

Saturday morning at breakfast the boys told their

father of the night's events. "Sounds to me as if you must have been followed and spied on at the Batter house," the detective said.

"Frank suspected someone was tailing us," Joe put in.

"Then when the thieves looked in through the windows," Mr Hardy went on, "they realized for the first time they hadn't taken *all* of Batter's stuffed animals. So they acted fast."

"And at least one of them came here to check our garage before we could get back home," Frank added. "Soapy Moran may have tipped them off about Chet's taxidermy work."

As they finished Aunt Gertrude's tasty flapjacks and sausages, Mr Hardy announced that he would be busy for most of the weekend on the Lektrex security check. "But I called the *Star* yesterday," he said, "and arranged to have them send us a copy of last Monday's edition from New York, special delivery. If you boys are around when it gets here, try decoding that first message you picked up."

Later, they telephoned Chet. His sister Iola answered. Iola, a pert brunette, was Joe's idea of the prettiest girl in Bayport.

"Chet and I have decided to give a party at our place tonight," she said. "Nothing special, just fun. Can you make it?"

"Sure thing," Joe said. "Count me in."

"Good! There'll be about a dozen, including Callie, of course."

"That'll make up Frank's mind," Joe said with a sly grin at his brother. Callie Shaw, an attractive blonde, was Frank's favourite date. "Is Chet there?" he asked.

"No." Iola giggled. "He took his staff of helpers fishing, to get a specimen to work on. He's coming to your house later. Oh, by the way, would you two pick up Biff Hooper? He doesn't get off from his watchman's job until eight, and his car is out of commission."

"Sure. We'll take the *Sleuth* and come by way of Willow River," Joe promised.

It was after one o'clock when Chet's yellow jalopy finally pulled into the driveway. Chet and the three youngsters were munching candy bars – a second dessert to their picnic lunch.

"Look what we caught!" Jimmy squealed proudly, holding up a five-pound black bass.

"Wait'll you see it mounted," Chest boasted. "Then it'll *really* look like something."

"Nice going," said Frank. Sensing an opportune moment, he told about the latest theft of Elias Batter's stuffed animals and proposed that Chet opened the aardvark and bear cub. "Whatever those thieves are after must be valuable," Frank argued. "Just think – you might find something in those animals that's worth a fortune!"

"And again I might not," Chet said with a pained look. "Then what do I have? Two ruined specimens, or else a big job sewing them up."

"So what? That ought to be a snap for an old maestro like Professor Morton," Joe put in.

Jimmy said nothing, but he shot an excited glance at the Hardys and then gazed at Chet.

"Look, you could do it at the party tonight," Frank wheedled as he saw Chet hesitating. "Have a grand opening before the whole gang – and display your fish masterpiece at the same time!"

The stout youth broke into a slow, pleased smile as he pictured Chet Morton, Taxidermist, dazzling the party guests with his exhibition of talent.

"Hmm! That's not a bad idea. Okay, I'll do it!"

Having detected an aroma of freshly baked cookies, Chet soon appeared in the kitchen, holding paste and newspaper to prepare some papier mâché. "May I borrow a bowl, Miss Hardy? Mmm, gee! Those cookies smell great!"

Aunt Gertrude frowned severely, her hands floury from the bread dough she was mixing. "Very well, you'll find another bowl like this one in the cupboard – and please leave a few cookies for our dinner tonight, Chet Morton!"

The copy of the *Star* arrived in mid-afternoon. Frank and Joe immediately set to work checking the page and column references from the first message. Meanwhile, Chet and his taxidermy crew were working earnestly in the garage.

While Jimmy cut a body form from half-inch board, Chet laid the fish on wet oilcloth, made a lateral incision, and peeled the body out of the skin with Mike and Tommy's help. While the two boys treated the skin with borax, Chet himself worked on the bass's head.

Later he came plodding up to the Hardy boys' bedroom to see how they were making out with the code message. Frank and Joe had already extracted three sentences from the paper:

> **Progress** *will certainly have to be stepped up if the bridge is to be completed on schedule.*
> *To curb such illegal betting* **activities**, *police will check all suspected bookmakers.*
> *The publicity* **flight** *will leave on Monday for Miami.*

Taking the third word after each code word, Frank assembled the entire message:

HAVE SHEEP CHECK ON HARES.

"Still pretty meaningless until we know whom 'sheep' and 'hares' stand for," Joe grumbled.

"Suppose – just suppose – that "hares' means the Hardys," Frank mused. "In other words, say this was an order for someone to check on *us* . . ."

Joe gasped. "Then "sheep' may be Soapy Moran! That's why he came snooping around the next day!"

There was a loud yell from outside. Chet raised the window. "What's the matter, Mike?"

"You sure that papier mâché's okay?" the urchin called up plaintively.

"Certainly, I'm sure," Chet retorted indignantly. "I made it, didn't I?"

"But it doesn't seem to go on right."

"Listen. Just trowel it on over the excelsior, as I told you! Don't you think I know what I'm talking about when it comes to taxidermy?"

"Well . . . okay . . . if you say so."

"And tell Jimmy to be melting the yellow petroleum

wax in the double boiler on the hot plate. I'll be down later to apply the finishing touches." Chet slammed the window, shaking his head. "Boy, it's not easy, teaching a fine art like taxidermy to a bunch of novices!"

"Sure you hadn't better go down there and keep an eye on things?" Joe, asked grinning.

"Don't worry, they know what to do. I've trained 'em pretty well, if I do say so myself." Chet yawned. "Besides, I need to lie down for a minute or two. Man, I was up at six this morning."

The Hardys chuckled as snores soon sounded through the room. Later, Joe shook Chet awake. "Hey, Maestro! Aunt Gertrude wants to know if you've seen her bowl of bread dough?"

"Huh! Bread dough?" Chet blinked sleepily. "All I know is, it was on the kitchen table when I took the papier mâché in the pantry – " The chubby youth's eyes widened and his jaw dropped as a horrible thought struck him.

He leapt to his feet and dashed downstairs. As he ran to the garage, Frank and Joe followed, scenting interesting developments.

The three youngsters greeted them with puzzled looks. "Hey, Chet," said Tommy, "somethings wrong with the fish. It looks like – well, like it's *growing*, or something!"

The shellacked bass had been placed in front of a glowing electric heater to dry. Its sides were visibly expanding! Chet groaned in dismay. "Oh, no-o-o!"

The grilled skin was puffing out like a balloon. One

stitch popped, then two, and a white paste tricked out the side.

"Good grief!" Joe exclaimed. "Don't tell me they used Aunt Gertrude's yeast dough instead of papier mâché?"

Chet nodded and sank down on a stool, covering his face with his hands. "Great, just great! It's all my fault! I picked up the wrong bowl!"

Frank and Joe were still chuckling over the incident that evening as they steered over the Willow River in their sleek motorboat, the *Sleuth*, to pick up Biff Hooper. Presently they came to the huddled buildings and high fences of the Lektrex plant. To their surprise, the entire area lay in darkness.

"That's funny," Frank murmured. "I wonder if there's been a power failure."

Their chum was not at the dock. Disturbed, the Hardy's tied up and jumped out to look for him. Suddenly a loud, clanging bell shattered the night stillness.

"The plant alarm!" Joe cried out. "Something's wrong!"

The Hardys leapt ashore and ran towards the main gate. Frank tripped on something in the darkness. His scalp prickling fearfully, he swung his flashlight beam downward. Both boys gasped as they saw the body of Biff Hooper lying bound and gagged on the ground!

Dock Attack

"Biff!" Frank cried out. As he dropped to a crouch beside the Hardys' motionless chum, his nostrils caught a sickish-sweet odour.

"Is he alive!" Joe asked fearfully.

"Seems to be breathing okay." Frank ripped off the gag. "My guess is he was chloroformed."

Almost as Frank spoke, they heard the roar of a motor. A car zoomed off in the darkness.

"Looks as if that second code message meant just what it said!" Joe murmured in a tense voice. "*Raid Lektrex plant!*"

"Get Biff untied," Frank said. "I'll try to phone for a doctor and the police!"

Springing to his feet, Frank dashed towards the plant. The new wing jutted out from the left of the main building. On the right, farther back, stood the powerhouse with its high smokestack. Frank tried the front door. It opened readily.

Inside, the light switch failed to work. Frank shone his flash around the pitch-dark lobby, then sucked in his breath. Another victim, an inside plant guard wearing a badge, lay unconscious on the floor. Like Biff, he had been tied and gagged.

Frank paused long enough to remove the man's gag

and unfasten his collar. Then he darked to the telephone on the reception desk and snatched it up. There was no dial tone.

From his previous visit to Lektrex, Frank new that the executive offices lay just beyond the lobby. He hurried down a corridor, probing with his flashlight. On the right was a large, glass-partitioned office with desks. At one end, his beam picked out a large safe. Its door was hanging loosely ajar!

Frank tried a phone on the desks. It, too was dead. He ran back outside to rejoin Joe. Biff was now stirring and moaning.

"He's coming to," Joe said.

"Good. The thieves cut both the phone lines and the lights." Frank told of the cracked safe and the unconscious guard. "I'll tend to him as soon as I alert the police over the boat radio."

He dashed back to the *Sleuth* and switched on their marine transceiver, using the police frequency. In moments he succeeded in making contact.

Frank was shutting off the radio when he heard a sudden noise. He whirled in time to see a dark figure spring on to the dock. Suddenly the man picked up a broken piece of planking and hurled it!

Though Frank ducked, the board struck him on the head with stunning force. He toppled backward in the boat.

Meanwhile, Joe was still working on Biff. The lanky youth's eyes opened and he struggled to sit up. "Easy, pal," Joe said soothingly. "How do you feel?"

"Sort of sickish. Guess I'll be all right, though, once I get over the wooziness."

The boys broke off as a man came running towards them out of the darkness. "That's Dan Cronin, one of the night guards," Biff said. "He's just coming on for the late shift."

Cronin took in the situation quickly. Biff, now well enough to talk, explained that he had been patrolling outside the plant when someone had seized him from behind and clamped a rag over his face. "That's all I remember."

"I figured something was wrong, even before I got here," Cronin said. He told the boys he had been walking along the river, on his way to work, when he heard the alarm go off. "But don't worry I've already kayoed one of the thugs. He was trying to get away in a boat."

"In a *boat*?" Joe's eyebrows shot up. "Good grief! That must've been my brother Frank!"

The words were hardly out of his mouth when a motobroat engine racketed into life. Joe leapt up and sped towards the dock with Cronin.

Too late! The *Sleuth* was already shooting out across the river. Joe's yell brought no answer.

"Are you sure that was your brother aboard?" Cronin asked.

"I don't know — I couldn't make out," Joe said, perplexed. "If that wasn't Frank, where is he?"

Both stared around the darkened shore area but could see no one. Puzzled ard worried, Joe walked back with Cronin to Biff, who was now on his feet. All three entered the plant to attend to the other guard.

Cronin's mate on the night shift soon arrived, and a police car pulled up at the plant a moment later. By this time the inside guard whom Frank had discovered was able to tell his story.

"I was making my rounds when all of a sudden the lights went out," he reported. "Turned out the phones were dead, too, so I hustled downstairs to check with Biff. As I came through the lobby, two guys jumped me – at least I *think* there were two. I never even got a look at 'em before they slapped a chloroform rag over my face."

Joe, who was growing increasingly worried over Frank, asked the squad-car sergeant to have Mr Hardy notified at once. "Even if my brother's okay," Joe explained, "Dad has taken on a security investigation for Lektrex, and I think he should know about the robbery."

"Sure thing." The sergeant nodded and told his driver to radio word to police headquarters. "Better have them alert Chief Collig, too."

While the police checked the safe for fingerprints and searched the plant, Joe and Biff went back to the riverfront to keeep watch. But neither Frank nor the *Sleuth* returned.

Meantime, the plant lights were restored. Mr Hardy and Police Chief Collig arrived within seconds of each other. Both men listened intently to the stories of all involved.

"Any idea how much was taken from the safe?" Collig asked the inside plant guard.

"No, sir. Only the cashier could tell you that, or maybe one of the management."

"I called Jason Warner, the president," Mr Hardy

put in. "He and his wife were out, but their maid thinks she can reach him."

Joe said, "Dad, I'm going out and try to raise Frank on your car's short-wave."

"Good idea, son. If the *Sleuth* doesn't respond, we'd better organize a search."

Twenty minutes of repeated calls brought no answer. As Joe reported failure, Mr Hardy's face became drawn and grim. He turned to Ezra Collig. "There's nothing to be gained by waiting. Frank may be in serious danger. I'd like to use the police launch."

"It's on the way," Collig said. "And I've already alerted the Coast Guard."

Presently the long, powerful launch came churning up to the dock. A spotlight blazed on its deckhouse. As Collig, Joe, Biff and Mr Hardy leapt aboard, the boat officer told his chief, "We just got a radiotelephone flash from the harbour master, sir. It may be a lead."

"Let's have it!" Collig snapped.

"A call came in from a cottager down at Green Point on the bay, just below the river mouth. Said he heard the noise of a motorboat putting in at a little brushy cove right next to his place. Seemed funny at this time of night, so he switched on his dock lights to try to see what was going on. He was just able to glimpse the boat as it went chugging away again."

"Who was in it!" the police chief demanded.

Joe's heart sank as the boat officer replied, "That's why he called, sir. Apparently there was *nobody* aboard."

·13·

A Tense Search

'You mean the boat had just been turned adrift?" Mr Hardy asked tensely.

"Evidently," the officer replied. "The cottager thought the boat might have been stolen and the thief was getting rid of it. That's why he reported the incident to the harbour master."

"He could be wrong," Collig cut in, noting the Hardys' worried looks. "At a distance in the dark he wouldn't be able to see too well. But we'll check it out."

At a barked command from him, the launch revved its engines and shot away. Joe and his father gripped the rail in silence as they sped down the river, gnawed by fear.

Was it the *Sleuth* the cottager had seen? And if so, what had happened to Frank? Had he been kidnapped by the gang? Biff said nothing but squeezed Joe's arm sympathetically.

The launch's powerful searchlight swept the river from bank to bank, glinting back from windows of houses along the shore. The river itself seemed bare of any craft.

"You saw no sign of a motorboat on your way up river?" Mr Hardy queried the boat officer.

"No, and we heard none, either. But the *Sleuth* could have reached the bay before we entered the river, couldn't it?"

Joe nodded. "Sure, there was plenty of time – if it headed that way."

"Which way do you *think* it headed?" Mr Hardy asked his son.

"Down river, from the sound of it. But it may have turned around after we went into the plant."

Reaching Barmet Bay, the police launch swung in the direction of Green Point. The crafts brilliant beam scanned the dark, oily waters.

"Look!" Biff yelled excitedly.

Far out on the bay he had just seen a pinpoint flash of light. Two more flashes stabbed the darkness in quick succession. Then came three long flashes, followed by three more short ones.

"SOS! Someone's signalling for help!" Joe exclaimed. "Let's go!"

The launch sheered around and sped towards the flashes. Its bow ripped the water into wings of spray. Presently their search beam picked out a familiar craft some distance ahead.

The *Sleuth!*

It was drifting sluggishly. A lone figure aboard waved a flashlight as they approached.

"Frank! Thank goodness he's safe!" Fenton Hardy muttered tensely.

The launch cut its engine and eased gently alongside. Joe tossed his brother a line to pull the two boats closer together. Then Frank scrambled up on the deck of the police craft.

"What happened, son?" Mr Hardy asked after embracing him.

"The whole thing's a mystery," Frank replied. "Someone conked me with a board back at the Lektrex dock. When I came to, I was drifting on the bay out of gas and the radio smashed."

"The plant watchman kayoed you by mistake," Joe explained. "He thought you were a robber."

"Then how come I wound up out here!" Frank asked in bewilderment. "Don't tell me I steered all the way down river unconscious!"

"No, I'd say one of the real gang must have sneaked aboard *after* you were knocked out," put in Mr Hardy. "He probably used the *Sleuth* to make his own getaway."

"That doesn't figure either, Dad." Frank frowned, then winced as he fingered the bruise on the side of his head. "Joe and I heard a car speed off right after we stumbled over Biff. That must have been the robbers' car."

"Could be. We'll figure it out later after we get you to a doctor." The investigator drew his son closer to the lighted deckhouse. "Let's have a look at your head."

Frank's scalp was only slightly cut and the bleeding had stopped, but a livid swelling had risen under his dark hair.

"May not be too bad, but we'd better have a physician examine you," Mr Hardy said. "Biff, you might do with some medical attention, too."

"I'll call for a squad car to stand by at the police wharf," Collig promised.

While the chief was speaking over the radio-telephone, Joe told his brother how a cottager had reported seeing a motorboat adrift near Green Point. "It was probably the *Sleuth* with you lying inside it."

"But who brought it down river from the plant?" Frank asked, puzzled.

"Let's go over the whole sequence of events," Mr Hardy suggested as Chief Collig emerged from the deckhouse. "You boys heard the alarm, then ran up to the plant, found Biff, and heard the car drive away. Is that how it happened?"

"That's right," Joe said. "The funny thing is the alarm and the sound of the car came only a couple of minutes apart. I don't see how they could have cracked the safe in that short time."

"No problem there," put in Collig. "What you fellows heard was an auxiliary alarm that was tripped when the safe door opened."

"Sure. The main alarm probably never went off at all," Biff added, "because they didn't break in. They used my keys."

"Then that explains everything!" Frank snapped his fingers excitedly. "One of the crooks must have been waiting in their car, keeping a lookout. I'll bet he panicked when he heard the safe alarm and saw Joe and me running up with our flashlights."

"So he scrammed in the car and left his partner, or partners, stranded inside the plant," Joe concluded.

"Right," said Frank. "And then whoever got left behind sneaked out the back door, spotted the *Sleuth*, and used that to make a getaway."

"Wow! You're lucky he didn't dump you overboard pal!" Biff commented.

Frank grinned wryly. "Maybe he figured I'd be more useful as a hostage if he ran into trouble."

Both Chief Collig and Mr Hardy agreed with the boys' reconstruction of the crime.

Meanwhile, the launch was proceeding back to Bayport Harbour at a fast clip, trailing the *Sleuth* behind it on a towline. A squad car was waiting when they tied up at the police wharf. Chief Collig, Fenton Hardy, and the boys all climbed in with its two officers, and the car sped off to Bayport Hospital.

Here the Hardys and Biff got out. The policemen continued on to the Lektrex plant. In the emergency room a doctor examined Biff and Frank. He dressed the latter's head injury and said that other than this, neither youth appeared to have suffered any ill effects.

"What about Iola's party?" Biff asked as they walked out of the hospital.

"I'm all for going," said Frank. "Okay, Dad?"

Mr Hardy hesitated. "Well . . . I think you'd both be better off in bed, but if you really feel up to it, I guess there's no objection. I'll go back to Lektrex and find out what was taken."

The boys debated whether to get Frank and Joe's convertible, parked near their boathouse, or refuel the *Sleuth* and go upriver to the landing stage near the Morton farm. Since they were already late, the group decided to take the car.

"We can drop Dad off on the way, and pick up the *Sleuth* tomorrow," said Joe.

The four taxied to the waterfront and transferred to

the convertible. Twenty minutes later they pulled up at the Lektrex plant. Jason Warner, who was just coming out to his own car, hailed the Hardys.

"Looks as though your warning about a raid was correct, boys," he said to Frank and Joe ruefully.

"Did they make much of a haul?" Joe asked.

"Not much. Luckily there was less than two hundred dollars in the safe."

"No technical material taken?" Fenton Hardy asked with a puzzled frown.

Warner shook his head. "So far as we can determine, no. Of course if they'd had time to comb through our engineering files, it might've been a different story. But even then it would have been hard for them to pick out what was important."

Frank had a sudden hunch. "What about that stuffed fox in your conference room, sir? Was it stolen?"

"The stuffed fox?" Warner stared at Frank. "Why, I really didn't notice."

"If you don't mind, I'd like to take a look."

All three youths piled out of the convertible and hurried into the plant with the two men. Jason Warner entered the conference room first and switched on the overhead fluorescent lights. An instant later his jaw dropped in astonishment.

The stuffed fox was gone!

14

Treasure Hunt

"Great Scott!" Warner looked as if he could hardly believe his eyes, on discovering that the stuffed fox was missing from its shelf.

Then swung around to Frank. "Young man, is this some kind of joke?"

"Of course not."

"Then how in the world did you know that the fox had been taken?" Warner demanded sharply.

"I didn't know. It was just a guess," Frank replied. "You see, a number of stuffed animals have been stolen around Bayport lately and Joe and I were asked to investigate. We still haven't discovered what's behind the thefts."

The Lektrex president frowned. "This case seems to be getting more mysterious by the minute. To begin with, I thought we were up against a ring of industrial spies. Instead, they crack the safe and steal our petty cash. And now you're talking about a series of stuffed animal robberies!"

"The same gang seems to be behind the animal thefts and the trade-secret espionage," said Fenton Hardy. "We don't know the connection yet, but there certainly must be one."

Warner gave a baffled shrug. "Well, let's hope some

clue can be gleaned from tonight's break-in that will help clear things up."

The boys left the plant to head for Iola and Chet's party. As they drove away, Joe shot a quizzical glance at his brother. "Do you suppose the thieves just happened to stumble on the fox during the robbery?"

"Stumble on it? No, sir!" said Frank. "If they just came to crack the safe, it's not likely they'd even have looked in the conference room. I'd be willing to bet the fox was their real motive and the safe-cracking just a cover-up."

"Listen, you guys! Clue me in, will you?" said Biff. "What gives with this stuffed animal racket? And why should a gang of thieves go to so much trouble to swipe a stuffed fox?"

"We're as much in the dark as you are," Frank said wryly. "Our guess is that one of the animals must contain something valuable. Maybe Chet'll crack the case for us tonight, if we're lucky."

Biff was excited after the Hardys had given him details. "Boy, what an evening! First a robbery and now a hidden treasure!"

The Morton farmhouse was aglow with light, and dance music from Iola's hi-fi came throbbing out on the crisp night air. As the Hardys' convertible pulled up, Chet popped on to the veranda to greet the three latecomers.

"Hey! What kept you guys so long? Iola and Callie wouldn't even let me serve the food till you got here! You want me to starve to death?"

"Starve!" Joe burst out laughing. "Listen, Chet,

you have enough surplus poundage stored up to hibernate for the winter!"

"Oh yeah! I'm down to a mere shadow from waiting for you slowpokes! What's your excuse?"

"Nothing special – just the crime of the century, that's all," Biff said casually.

"Crime of the century!" Iola gasped. Callie Shaw, Tony Prito, Phil Cohen, and the other party guests came crowding around the doorway as the boys entered. "What do you mean?"

"I got chloroformed, the Lektrex plant got looted, and Frank got kidnapped."

"*What!*" There was an explosion of questions from all sides. The teenagers listened and chattered excitedly as Biff and the Hardys related their night's harrowing adventures.

When the boys finished, Callie linked her arm through Frank's and led him to an easy chair. "What you need is some rest and refreshment. How about some fruit punch to start with?"

"Aaah!" Frank sank down with a contented grin.

"Double portion!"

Iola was fixing cushions on the sofa for Joe and Biff. "Someone pass those appetizers, please. Chet, you get busy on the hamburgers!"

"Now you're talking, Sis!" The chubby youth went bounding towards the kitchen.

Soon the party was in full swing again. Games and more dancing followed the refreshments. Finally the moment arrived for the "grand opening" of Chet's bear and aardvark. But before he could make the necessary preparations, his friends started to needle him about his rising-dough fish.

The young taxidermist took the ribbing good-naturedly. "Okay, funny folks." He set down his tools and rubbed his hands briskly. "Let's clear a little work space here!"

Newspapers were spread on the living-room floor, and the two stuffed animals set in the centre. With professional flare Chet donned an apron and opened his taxidermy kit.

"Do you really think there could be a treasure inside one of them?" Callie asked eagerly.

"It's just a hunch," Joe murmured.

"Chet, are you sure you'll be able to put the beasts together again?" Iola queried.

"Sure, nothing to it!" Chet gave the aardvark a last affectionate pat. "Hate to do this, old boy, but you're in the best professional hands."

Turning the animal on its side, the pudgy craftsman opened his taxidermy kit and began work like a surgeon. Tony Prito assisted.

"Medium scalpel."

"Medium scalpel!" Tony echoed, slapping the instrument into Chet's outstretched hand.

"Paring knife."

"Paring knife!"

"Small surgical scissors and hammer."

"Small surgical scissors and hammer!"

Working with deft strokes, Chet carefully opened the underside of the aardvark. The job proved more difficult than expected. As he removed a section of the inner shell structure, a hush fell over the party guests.

Frank and Joe watched impatiently, fingers crossed. Were they on the verge of solving the baffling mystery of the Batter estate?

With the opening large enough, Chet's hands probed the entire length of the aardvark. He removed the excelsior, then shook the animal. Nothing more came out!

"It's empty!" Chet's face was a picture of comical disappointment.

"Never mind! maybe the secret's inside the bear!" Frank said hastily, fearing their stout chum might lose heart for the task.

"Okay, but this had better not be a wild-goose chase!"

"How can you chase a wild goose inside a stuffed bear!" piped up a boy named Jerry Gilroy.

"You want me to use this scalpel on *you?*" Chet waved it menacingly as the girls giggled.

Half an hour later the bear cub, too, had been thoroughly probed without result.

"Of all the dopey ideas – !" Chet glared at the Hardys. "Just for that I ought to make you two brilliant Sherlocks sew up these specimens!"

"We'd be glad to," Joe said soothingly, "but don't you see, doctor, we lack your professional – Oof!"

Howls of laughter went up as a wad of excelsior caught Joe squarely in the face. But Chet's good nature was soon restored, and the floor was cleared again for more dancing.

Next day, over Sunday dinner, Frank and Joe discussed the baffling case with their father.

"We know," said Frank, "that the gang found

nothing in the animals they stole from the auction *or* in the wolf's head. Otherwise, they wouldn't have taken the rest of the animals Friday night."

"And now *we* know Batter hid nothing in the aardvark or bear cub," Joe added.

"Right! Which leaves one possibility," Frank went on. "That stuffed fox taken from Lektrex."

"But if Warner's right, Batter never mounted that specimen," said Mr Hardy, frowning.

"We can't be sure, Dad," Frank argued. "All he said was that he got it from a friend in New York. Since the gang stole the fox, they may have some reason for connecting it with Batter."

Fenton Hardy nodded thoughtfully. "All right, that's a reasonable assumption to work on."

"I think we should call Mr Warner," said Frank, "and check up on the person who gave him the fox."

Frank reached him by telephone at his home. "Mr Warner, would you mind telling me the name of the friend who gave you the stuffed fox?" Frank asked.

"A fellow named Nils Afron. He's a wealthy interior decorator in New York City. Does office décor." Warner said he did not know Afron well and had met him on a hunting trip in Canada.

"Could you give me his address, please?"

"Hmm. I don't have it with me, but my secretary can look it up tomorrow and phone you."

"We'd appreciate that, sir." After hanging up, Frank suggested to his father that someone should go to New York and interview Afron.

"I agree, son, but this security check has me pretty well tied up for the next few days. How would you boys like to fly to New York tomorrow and see him? You could get excused from school early."

Joe gave a whoop. "Great idea, Dad!"

The following afternoon Frank and Joe left school at one o'clock. They stopped at their house to get Afron's address from Aunt Gertrude, then drove to the airport. Two hours later their plane was touching down at La Guardia Field.

After riding to the East Side Air Terminal in Manhattan, the brothers walked to Forty-Second Street and caught a crosstown bus.

"Wonder if we should have phoned first to make sure Afron's in," Joe murmured.

Frank shook his head. "Better to catch him off-guard, I'd say. Then if he does know anything about Batter or the gang, he'll have no time to cover up, or invent a story."

They got off the bus at the Avenue of the Americas and walked quickly to their destination in the West Forties. The address proved to be a small, grimy-looking office building.

"Not a very classy place for a wealthy decorator to have his studio," Joe said in surprise.

Inside, they consulted the wall directory, listing the firms with offices in the building. Afron's name was not among them. Frank turned to the uniformed elevator dispatcher who was standing nearby at his post in the lobby.

"Could you tell us the office number of Afron Business Décor, please?"

"Afron Business Décor?" The dispatcher frowned and shrugged. "Never heard of it. There's no such outfit in this building."

15

Mystery Scrambler

No decorating firm on the premises!

"The owner's name is Nils Afron," Joe told the elevator dispatcher. "You're sure he's not located at this address?"

"Not since I've been here, Bud. You can see for yourself – his name's not on the board."

"How long *have* you been working here?" Frank spoke up.

"About a month and a half."

"Then it's possible Afron might have had an office here before you came and moved out?"

"Can't prove it by me." The dispatcher gestured towards a door at the far end of the lobby. "Try Mr Smith, the manager, over there. He'd know."

"Thanks, we will," said Frank.

The boys knocked on the door and were told to come in. A stout, elderly man was seated at a desk inside. He listened patiently to their query, then nodded.

"There was an Afron Business Décor on the third floor. Closed up a couple of months ago."

"Did Mr Afron leave any forwarding address?" Joe asked.

"No. Just went out of business, I guess." The

manager removed his glasses, breathed on the lenses, and polished them briskly. "Can't say I was surprised. Only a small setup. Never seemed to have any customers."

"Can you tell us anything about him?" Frank persisted. "Anything that might help us locate him?"

Mr Smith peered at the boys suspiciously, "Didn't he pay his bills? Are you skip tracers or something?"

Frank said, "No, but we think Afron may have information that would help solve a robbery."

"Hmm. Well, I'm afraid I can't tell you much. Like I say, he had only a small suite here. A few office furnishings on display. I don't believe he even had a secretary."

"What did he look like?" Joe asked curiously.

"Big blond fellow, about forty, I'd say. Close-cut curly hair and sort of a pug nose. Always dressed and talked like a million bucks, though."

"Well, thanks very much." Frank took out one of Fenton Hardy's business cards. "If Afron shows up here again for mail or any other reason, will you please call us collect?"

Mr Smith looked impressed when he saw the famous detective's name. "You bet I will, son."

Frank and Joe flew back to Bayport, eager to report on their trip. Both felt there was something odd about the circumstances surrounding Nils Afron which might bear looking into.

It was past six o'clock in the evening when their convertible pulled into the driveway. Aunt Gertrude, whom they had phoned from the airport, was setting the table for dinner.

"Where's Dad?" Joe asked eagerly.

"He was called over to the Lektrex Company an hour ago, and with the roast already in the oven. Something urgent, it seems." Aunt Gertrude sniffed audibly as she smoothed the tablecloth. "These big businessmen seem to think they're the only people with problems. Never occurs to them that cooking a meal entails a few problems, too!"

Frank asked, "Any idea what it was about?"

"Not the slightest."

Frank and Joe went upstairs to get ready for dinner. Later, as they were eating, Joe asked Frank, "Do you think we should wait until Dad gets home to tell him about Afron or should we call him?"

Frank frowned uncertainly. "I've been wondering that myself. If something new has come up on the plant robbery, our information on Afron might be an important lead."

"Then let's call him right after dinner."

As soon as they finished dessert, Frank dialled the Lektrex number. He asked the plant operator to locate his father and was switched to Jason Warner's office.

Fenton Hardy was very much interested in their news. "I'd certainly like to know more about this fellow Afron," he commented. "I have a feeling that stuffed fox may be the key to this whole mystery."

The detective paused. "Tell you what. You and Joe have been mixed up in this Lektrex case from the outset. Suppose you boys drop over here and sit in on this meeting."

"We'll leave right away," Frank promised.

When they arrived at the plant, the young sleuths

were conducted to the conference room adjoining Mr Warner's office. Mr Hardy was seated at the conference table with the president and several other key executives of the company. Places were made for Frank and Joe.

"We're no longer dealing with a simple case of robbery." Jason Warner informed them. "Our latest technical development has been pirated by a foreign electronics firm in Hong Kong."

"That new thin-film circuitry?" Frank asked.

"Exactly. We just learned this Hong Kong firm is exporting a similar product." Warner added angrily, "The details of their circuitry are identical with ours – it can't be a coincidence!"

"What about technical journals?" put in Fenton Hardy. "Could they have picked up clues from scientific papers your staff has written?"

"Not a chance," snapped the chief engineer. "The main feature depends on a new high-vacuum technique for vapourizing metals, and we've kept that under tight wraps."

The boys learned that all blueprints, research data, and other written material had been checked and that no copies were missing.

"Then the only possible answer seems to be a disloyal employee," Mr Hardy said. "Before we go into that angle, though, you might like to hear what my sons discovered in New York today."

Frank and Joe told about Afron's business setup and how he had moved out, leaving no forwarding address.

"Did you try the telephone company?" Mr Hardy asked.

"Yes, Dad, we called from the airport," Frank replied. "The operator checked all the New York boroughs. Neither Afron nor his decorating company are listed anywhere."

Jason Warner frowned. "Seems odd, I'll agree, but I still don't see how it ties in with a security leak here at Lektrex."

"You said you met Afron on a hunting trip?" Joe asked.

"Yes. We stayed at the same place – the Lachine Hunting Lodge on Lake Okemow in Ontario. It caters to wealthy businessmen. There were only a few other guests at the lodge. Naturally we got acquainted."

"How did he happen to give you the stuffed fox?" Frank asked.

"Afron came through Bayport on a business trip a couple of weeks later," Warner explained. "He stopped in my office for a chat and that's when he presented it to me. Just a sales gimmick for getting his foot in the door, I suppose. He was evidently hoping to wangle a contract to redecorate our executive offices."

Mr Hardy said with a faint smile, "But you didn't fall for his sales approach?"

Warner shrugged. "He pussyfooted around and suggested redoing my suite and the conference room in an outdoor sportsman style. But he was barking up the wrong tree. We had no plans to redecorate. I left the fox on the shelf where he placed it and forgot the whole thing."

The Lektrex sales manager proposed that all technical employees be given a lie-detector test. Fenton Hardy promised to arrange one the next morning. Presently Frank and Joe excused themselves from the meeting and left the plant.

Before tackling their homework that evening, the boys cross-checked their father's criminal file for likely suspects. They could find no one who seemed to fit Afron's description.

By ten o'clock Mr Hardy still had not returned from the Lektrex Company. Frank and Joe went up to their attic radio shack for some ham transmission before going to bed. They were monitoring the 2-metre band when a sudden burst of gibberish came from the speaker.

"Hold it!" Joe exclaimed, and Frank's fingers froze on the tuning knob. The garbled, voice-like sounds continued in a jerky staccato sequence. "It's that scrambler again – the same one we heard the night Chet pulled his apeman stunt!"

Frank nodded, listening intently. "Let's hang on till they sign off so we can get their call letters."

For several minutes the gibberish continued. Then abruptly the speaker became silent. The transmission had ended with no identification!

Frank cried out, "That was definitely an illegal broadcast, Joe!"

"Right! And we know the Aardvark gang uses radio in their operations!"

The brothers were excited by the same thought: *Had they stumbled on another secret broadcast by the industrial spy ring?*

16

On the Beam!

"One thing doesn't add up, Joe," Frank pointed out. "If the gang sends messages in that code we cracked, why would they need a scrambler?"

"Maybe they're wise to the fact that we've solved the code – or anyhow they *think* we've solved it, from the way we showed up at Lektrex Saturday night. So now they're switching to a scrambler."

Frank shook his head. "Can't be. We picked up the other scrambler broadcast before we ever heard them talk in code."

"That's right. I forgot." Joe scowled and rubbed his jaw thoughtfully. "Okay, how about this? Maybe the newspaper code is for long-range messages – such as orders from the boss of the gang in some other city."

"The boss being Aardvark himself?"

"Right. The scrambler is used for local stuff – you know, like fast two-way conversations they don't have time to put in code."

"That might be the answer," Frank conceded. "We still don't know, though, if both broadcasts were by the gang. But it's a cinch that whoever is using the scrambler is up to something crooked."

"Sure! They're using it illegally on a ham band and

they're giving no call letters – which makes a double violation of FCC rules. No honest ham would dare risk losing his licence."

The boys brooded silently for a few moments. Then Frank looked up at his brother.

"You know, Joe, I think you just put your finger on something."

"Such as?"

"Using that scrambler could be risky for the gang. It might get the FCC on their tail."

"It sure could," Joe agreed drily. "But so what?"

"So if they have any brains, they're probably using this only for short-range communication at very low power."

Joe's eyes suddenly lit up as he realized what Frank was thinking. "But we were receiving it loud and clear – which may mean they're transmitting right in our area!"

"Check! We've been meaning to run a field-strength test on our transmitter," Frank went on. "Why don't we do it tomorrow after school, and while we're at it, we can listen in for the scrambler again. With luck, we might even get some notion from what direction it's coming."

Joe nodded enthusiastically. "Good idea. We can get Chet to operate our rig here at the house."

Tuesday morning, when they broached the matter to Chet at school, he agreed willingly to help out in the test. "I usually get hungry about that time of day, though," the stout boy warned. "Do any rations go with the job."

Frank chuckled. "I guess Aunt Gertrude won't mind fixing a few sandwiches."

That afternoon Chet manned the attic transmitter while Frank and Joe cruised around the outskirts of Bayport in their convertible.

"Where are you now?" Chet called from the house.

"Rockcrest Drive near the foot of Mound Road," Joe radioed.

"How's my signal?"

"You're S-9," Joe said, indicating that Chet was coming through at maximum signal strength.

"Okay, keep going around those western hills," Chet replied. "Give me another reading when you get down by Surprise Lake."

Minutes later Joe reported, "Now your signal's dropped off to S-4."

"Roger. Try me again when you get near Highway 10."

The test continued. Between their reports to Chet, Joe switched their car receiver to the frequency on the 2-meter band over which they had heard the scrambler the previous night. Nothing supicious came over the speaker until they had circled the northern outskirts of town and were heading back towards the bay on a route that parallelled the Willow River. Then, suddenly, the voice gibberish crackled in strongly!

"It's peaking right along here!" Joe exclaimed as he watched the meter needle swing sharply towards maximum strength.

As they drove along, however, the scrambler sounds soon faded and the needle dropped again.

"That's funny," Joe said. "Something must be

cutting it off." He glanced around, but could see no obvious obstruction in the terrain that might have interfered with the signal.

"Wait a second. Let's go back and try it again." Frank turned the convertible and retraced the stretch of road over which they had just travelled. Again the gibberish burst in loud and clear!

"The signal must be coming in a fairly narrow beam," Frank deduced.

"But what direction?"

Frank pulled over to the side of the road and asked Joe to hand him the Bayport map from the glove compartment. "We know we picked up the signal pretty clearly at home," Frank said, indicating with a pencil the position of their house on Elm Street, "and we know we're receiving it good right here."

"I get it," Joe put in eagerly. "If they're transmitting between fixed points, the beam must run roughly – let's see – about east-southeast to west-northwest."

"Check." Frank ruled an approximate line to indicate the beam. "Let's weave back and forth on some of the dirt roads east of here, and see if we keep picking up the signal on the same line."

As Frank started the car again, Joe switched back to their previous test frequency and told Chet what they intended to do. For the next twenty minutes, their convertible rambled to and fro over several roads and country lanes while the Hardys listened carefully for the gibberish sounds.

Their theory was quickly borne out as the sounds came in clearly, then faded again. The scrambler broadcast was evidently being transmitted more or less along the line which Frank had pencilled.

"So far so good," Joe concluded. "But how do we zero in on the source? All we know is that the beam runs between Bayport and the Willow River."

"The Willow River!" Frank suddenly braked the car and reached for the map. "Joe, we're a couple of dummies! Look here on the map. The answer's staring us right in the face!"

"What do you mean!"

"Don't you see where the beam intersects the river?" Frank jabbed the spot with his pencil. "That's where the Lektrex plant is located!"

Joe's lips puckered into an excited whistle. "Good night! Someone must be broadcasting from inside the plant! The spy who's been spilling technical secrets to the gang!"

"Looks that way. But let's check it out and make sure."

After a quick scrutiny of roads on the map, Frank steered the car on a zigzag route that gradually brought them closer to the electronics company. Although there were slight pauses now and then in the transmission, as if two or more speakers were conducting a conversation, the boys managed to pick up the gibberish sounds almost every time their route crossed the beam.

At last they reached the River Road which ran directly past the plant buildings. Once again they were unable to hear the scrambler. Frank pulled off the road, near the main gate, and the two young radio sleuths listened for several minutes, but their transceiver remained silent.

Joe gave his brother a quizzical look. "The spy must have signed off."

"I guess so." Frank heaved a sigh of disappointment. "What a tough break, just when we had a chance of nailing him!"

"I'd better call Chet," said Joe, "and let him know how we made out."

He started to tune the receiver back to their test frequency on a different band. But his fingers, twirling the knob, suddenly stiffened as a familiar voice came in faintly:

"This list covers all the engineers and technical employees working in the new wing, does it?"

"That's Dad!" Joe gasped.

Jason Warner's voice was replying:

"Yes. Of course there are the regular production workers to consider, but I think we can assume that none of them would have enough knowledge of the overall product to betray much to the spy ring."

Frank stared in amazement as the radio conversation continued. "Straight voice now – without the scrambler. I don't get it, Joe."

"Maybe someone switched off the scrambler."

"But this is over a different frequency!"

"Right! I'm goofing off again." Joe scratched his head, utterly mystified. "Let's backtrack and try farther away from the plant again."

"Okay. Good idea." Frank started the car, and after turning around, swung back up the dirt lane by which they had approached the River Road. The faint radio voices quickly faded.

As they angled across the path of the beam, Frank stopped the car and said, "Switch back to the 2-metre."

Joe did so. Once more the gibberish sounds of the scrambler could be heard! Frank opened the door abruptly and got out of the car.

"Where are you going!" Joe asked.

"I have an idea."

The dirt lane traversed an area of uncultivated field, overgrown with clumps of brush and occasional trees. By line of sight the distance from their present position to the spot where they had parked on the River Road across from the plant was only a few hundred yards.

Frank aligned his gaze approximately with the path of the radio beam. Then he strode across the field, cutting straight towards the plant. Joe watched and saw his brother finally come to a halt facing a gnarled old oak tree. Nearby it were several younger trees still clad in withered brown leaves.

With mounting excitement, Joe saw Frank leap up and hook his fingers into a hollow opening in the trunk, to hoist himself off the ground.

Moments later, Frank lowered himself again and shouted through cupped hands:

"Come quick, Joe! I've solved the mystery!"

17

Window Bug

In response to Frank's call, Joe dashed across the brush-strewn field. "What did you find?" he asked eagerly.

"There's some kind of radio rig inside this hollow oak. Here! I'll boost you up so you can see."

Frank held out clasped hands to form a stirrup for Joe's foot. Putting one hand on his brother's shoulder, Joe was hoisted up until his face was level with the hollow opening in the trunk.

"Wow! What a setup!" As Joe lifted his gaze, he gave another excited gasp. He had just noticed a cable protruding from another opening farther up the trunk. His eyes followed the cable upward.

"Frank, look!" Joe pointed to a small, square-horn antenna, positioned in a crotch of the tree and almost unnoticeable against the bark. "That's what's transmitting the beam!"

Joe dropped to the ground and faced his brother tensely. "The assembly in this tree must be a relay setup to catch the voice broadcast from the plant. Right?"

"Sure, the plant's bugged with a hidden mike and transmitter," Frank reasoned "It broadcasts conversation from somewhere inside the buildings. I'll bet this rig in the tree picks up the voice broadcast, amplifies and scrambles it, then beams it out at a higher frequency."

Joe gave a quick nod. "So what's our next move?"

"Dad must be at the plant right now," Frank said. "We'd better go warn him and Mr Warner pronto!"

The boys drove to the Lektrex Company and told the receptionist in the lobby that they must see their father. It was urgent. A guard took them to the executive conference room, where Mr Hardy had been reporting to Jason Warner and his personnel manager the results of the lie-detector tests.

"What's wrong, sons?" the detective asked.

For answer Frank put a finger to his lips, then wrote on a pad, "There's plenty wrong. How long have you and Mr Warner been talking in this room?"

Mr Hardy wrote, "For the past hour. Why?"

"The room's bugged!" Frank wrote. "We could hear your voices on the convertible's short-wave!"

Warner gaped in consternation as the Hardy boys took turns in writing their check on the scrambler and their discovery in the hollow oak.

"This is outrageous!" the president spluttered. He buzzed his secretary on the intercom. Before the Hardys could caution him to lower his voice, Warner ordered her to have an engineer bring detection equipment at once.

Within minutes the concealed 'bug' had been located. Using a sensitive electronic probe, the engineer quickly traced it to a wooden valance across the top of the picture-window drapery. The bug had been mounted on a small rack screwed to the inside of the valance.

"It's no amateur job, that's a cinch," the engineer, said admiringly. "It's one of the cleverest devices I've ever seen."

He pointed out the delicate electronic components, nestled in a small crystal-plastic block. "This monosyllabic detector responds only to human voice frequencies. In other words, it turns the bug on only when someone is speaking – and a delay circuit turns it off again when the conversation ceases."

"That's to prevent power draining from the batteries?" Fenton Hardy asked.

"Partly that, and it lessens the danger of detection too. If the bug were on all the time, there'd be too much risk of its being traced."

Taking along a ladder, the engineer accompanied Frank and Joe to the oak tree in the field across the plant. He removed the radio assembly from the tree and they carried it back to the conference room. Battery-powered, it consisted of a receiver-transmitter, a compact frequency flip-flop type scrambler, and the small directional horn antenna which Joe had spotted, connected to the transmitter by coaxial cable.

"The bug itself is fairly weak," the engineer explained. "It probably broadcasts only for a short distance outside the plant. This rig extends the broadcast range maybe up to four or five miles."

Fenton Hardy nodded thoughtfully. "And I suppose by transmitting the signal in a fairly narrow beam they cut down the chance of it being monitored by the FCC."

"FCC or hams, either one," the engineer replied. "Of course this conference room's used mostly at night. But if anyone did overhear the broadcast, as your sons did, the scrambler would keep them from guessing where it came from."

"I can't understand it." Still flustered and mystified, Jason Warner paced about the room with a frown. "If this was the source of the leak, how did our Hong Kong rival get into production so fast? The bug can only have been here a couple of weeks."

"How do you know that, sir?" Joe questioned.

"I remember the drapes were dry-cleaned late in October and the valance was repainted at the same time. If the bug was here before, it would have been discovered."

"Wait a moment!" Mr Hardy put in tensely. "We're forgetting the raid on the plant Saturday night. The bug may have been planted then, under cover of the robbery."

Frank shook his head. "We know the bug was already in operation then. The first time Joe and I heard the scrambler broadcast was more than a week before the robbery."

"Hmm." The detective's face took on a puzzled scowl. "In that case, there may be another bug that we haven't found yet. Jason, you'd better have your engineers check over the whole plant – especially the new wing."

The Lektrex president nodded. "I'll attend to it right away. Meantime, I'd like you to run lie-detector tests on *all* our employees. Start with our custodia crew – janitors, maintenance men, and so on. One of them may have been bribed to plant the bug."

Next day in the school lunchroom Frank and Joe were startled to hear their names called over the public-address system. The boys hastily finished their meal and hurried towards the principal's office.

"Wonder what's up," Joe murmured uneasily.

"Don't know. I sure hope everything's all right at home."

To their surprise, Fenton Hardy was waiting to see them.

"Dad!" Frank exclaimed. "Is anything wrong?"

"Yes and no." Mr Hardy gave a quick, reassuring smile. "How would you two like to handle an out-of-town job for me?"

"Great!" the boys chorused, and Joe added. "What's it all about?"

"Tell you on the way. Get your things and let's go. I've already taken the liberty of having you excused from the rest of your classes."

As the three strode through the hall, the investigator said he had had a sudden call from the Noltan Medical Company, a drug firm in Philadeliphia. "The formula for a new wonder drug they're producing has leaked out. A German firm has just put an indentical product on the market."

"Another Aardvark spy job?" Joe blurted.

"Looks very much that way," said Mr Hardy, "though, of course, there's always an outside chance that it's pure coincidence. I told John Noltan, the president, that my regular operatives and I were tied up here, but that I'd send you two to get the facts from him."

Frank flushed with pleasure at his father's confidence, but asked a bit uncertainly, "Did he object? To your sending us, I mean."

"Not at all. He's heard of you, and I told him you'd been working with me on a similar case here in Bayport."

Mr Hardy had already booked two seats on a one-thirty airline flight. The boys drove to the airport, left their convertible in the parking lot, and were soon boarding a sleek jet. An hour later it landed at the Philadelphia airfield.

Frank and Joe caught a taxi to the modernistic plant of the Noltan Medical Company. Mr Noltan, a burly man in a tweed suit, greeted them with a firm handshake.

"I assume your father has told you about our pirated drug formula," he began. "Please sit down and I'll – "

Noltan broke off abruptly in midsentence. "Is something wrong?" he queried.

The boys were staring past him, startled looks on their faces!

18

The Shaggy Spy

'Excuse us for staring, sir," Frank told Mr Noltan. "I think my brother noticed the same thing I did – that head up on the wall."

Frank gestured towards a huge, horned bison's head mounted on a wall plaque. The animal's glittering eyes seemed to stare out broodingly from under its dark furry topknot, and a woolly beard hung from its chin.

"You see, stuffed animals have kept cropping up in our investigation back in Bayport," Joe explained. "It seems odd to find one here, too."

"May we take the head down from the wall and examine it?" Frank asked.

Mr Noltan gave the boys a puzzled smile. "Very well, if you think it's important. I must say, I fail to see the point."

The Hardys managed to unhook the plaque and lift down the heavy head. Then Frank pushed aside the bison's beard and fingered the throat fur until he laid bare a row of stitches.

Joe gasped. "The same kind of workmanship we saw on the stuffed fox!"

Frank glanced up at the president of the drug firm and inquired, "Have you ever heard of a man named Elias Batter?"

Noltan shook his head. "Never."

"Where did you get this bison, sir?" Joe put in.

"It was presented to me by a friend."

"Was his name Afron?"

Noltan's jaw dropped in astonishment. "That's the man! Nils Afron. But how did you guess?"

"There was a stuffed fox stolen from the Lektrex plant in Bayport," Joe explained. "That animal was given to the president of the company by the same person, Nils Afron. Frank and I tried to check on him in New York but – "

"The Afron I know is an interior decorator," Noltan broke in. "He specializes in business office work. Let me see – I have his card right here." Noltan drew out a wallet, leafed through its contents, and handed a small business card to Joe. "There's his address."

"That *was* his address, sir," Joe said. "Frank and I learned he went out of business."

Noltan stared at the boys, utterly mystified.

"We've been working on the theory that one of these animals may have something valuable hidden inside it," Frank said. He shot a quizzical look at his brother. "But I think now we both have a *different* hunch."

"We sure do!" Joe said eagerly. "May we open up this bison head, Mr Noltan?"

"By all means! I don't know what you hope to find, but I'm just as curious as you are!" He handed Frank a pair of desk shears.

In a few minutes Frank had sliced through the stitching and the inner shell, and was probing inside the bison head. Suddenly his eyes flashed with excitement. When he withdrew his hand, he was clutching a compact electronic assembly! The boys' hunch had been correct!

Noltan stifled an angry gasp. "Is that gadget what I think it is?"

"If you mean an electronic bug," Frank replied, "you're right. This bison has been eavesdropping on everything said in your office."

"Where did you meet Afron, sir?" Joe queried.

"On a hunting trip in Northern Canada."

"At the Lachine Hunting Lodge on Lake Okemow?"

Noltan nodded bitterly. "You seem to know the whole story."

Frank said, "And later Afron came to visit you here and gave you the buffalo head?"

"Yes, he stopped in once when he was passing through Philadelphia." Noltan's face was red with rage at the way he had been tricked. "I assumed he was angling for a decorating job – but it seems he was after a bit more than that!"

"You're not his only victim," Frank said sympathetically. "The presdient of Lektrex was fooled the same way."

"It's probably Afron's regular method of operation," said Joe.

Noltan frowned. "But I though you said a stuffed fox was *stolen* from Lektrex. If so, how do you know it was bugged?"

"We don't, but it's a pretty safe bet." Frank told about the Saturday night raid on Lektrex plant, and the finding of a newly planted bug behind the window valance. "Chances are the new bug was installed during the robbery to replace the old one inside the fox."

Joe snapped his fingers. "And this makes better sense out of the code message, Frank!"

"How do you mean?"

"Don't you see? The message said: *Raid Lektrex plant new setup*. We thought it was all one sentence, meaning to raid the new plant wing. Actually it was two sentences, meaning to raid Lektrex *and* to plant a new bug!"

"Wow! That must be it, all right!" Frank paced about, unable to control is excitement. "Mr Noltan, may I use your phone! I'd like to report to Dad right away."

Noltan smiled wryly and gestured towards his desk. "It's the least I can do after the fast way you two have cracked this case!"

"We still don't have Afron and his gang, sir, but I'd say we're one step closer."

Frank dialled the long-distance operator and succeeded in reaching his father at the Lektrex plant. Mr Hardy was thrilled over his sons' successful detective work.

"You and Joe have done a great job! I'm proud of you," he told Frank. "The first scrambled broadcast you picked up must have come from the bug in the fox, and the code message confirms that the new bug was planted during the robbery – so we can call off the lie-detector tests."

Mr Hardy added that the boys should leave any

search for a scrambler near the Noltan Medical Company to the Philadelphia police and the FBI.

"By the way, Dad," Frank asked," is Chief Collig taking any steps to find the gang's listening post in Bayport?"

"Yes, he has squads of police out combing every block in town within the path of the radio beam. But as you know, that covers a lot of territory. The search may take days. I'm not too hopeful, especially since the gang must know we've discovered the bug."

Before hanging up, Frank suggested that his father have the FBI check all other firms which had suffered trade-secret leaks to see if they, too, had stuffed animals.

"Good idea, son. I'll do that."

The boys managed to get seats on a six-o'clock flight to Bayport. As they were eating dinner on the plane, Joe said, "There's one thing we still haven't figured out, Frank."

"What's that?"

"Why did Afron have his gang yank the fox out of the Lektrex plant?"

"Hmm. Good question." Frank gazed thoughtfully out the window at the twinkling lights of a town far below. "Maybe they got worried about us checking into the stuffed animal angle while Dad was investigating these industrial spy cases. If he was called to Lektrex, there was a danger we might put two and two together."

"Could be," Joe conceded. "But that still wouldn't explain the other animal thefts."

"No, you're right, it wouldn't." Frank added,

"Maybe we'd better not give up too soon on Jimmy Gordon's treasure hunt."

When the boys arrived home, they settled down in the living room with their father to discuss the latest developments in the case.

"The FBI called back a few minutes ago and reported on five firms," Mr Hardy said. "Three of them, including that California aircraft manufacturer, had bugged animals in their offices, and two had stuffed sailfishes."

"Did the FBI find out where the specimens came from?" Frank asked eagerly.

Mr Hardy nodded as he filled his pipe. "The animals had been presented as a gift by Nils Afron. In every case, a company executive had met him at a hunting lodge in Canada. The sailfishes came from a man named Neil Aaron. In those two cases, an acquaintance had been struck up during a fishing jaunt in Florida."

"Neil Aaron!" Joe exclaimed. "I'll bet that's just an alias for Nils Afron."

"No doubt about it," Mr Hardy agreed. "The description tallies exactly."

The telephone rang and Joe bounced up to answer it. "This is Chief Collig," said the caller. "We've just picked up Soapy Moran."

Moran – the small-time swindler who had worked for Elias Batter!

Joe's pulse quickened at the news. "That's great, Chief! Where is he?"

"We have him here at headquarters and I think

he's about ready to talk. I thought you boys and your dad might want to be here."

"We sure do! We'll be right down."

The Hardys sped off in the boys's convertible and pulled up outside the grey stone building that housed Bayport Police Headquarters.

In the interrogation room Soapy Moran was seated on a chair facing Chief Collig, two detectives, and an FBI agent. The gaunt swindler looked ready to wilt under the blazing light and their relentless questioning.

"You're free to call a lawyer," Collig told him.

"Never mind. I've told you all I know," Moran whined. He mopped beads of perspiration from his face. "Just give me a break, will you?"

"What has he confessed to?" Frank asked.

"I've admitted I conned your pal out of ten bucks," Moran said hastily. "Here – give it back to him." Whipping out a wallet, he extracted a ten dollar bill and laid it on the table.

"Tell them about the work you did for Elias Batter," Collig prodded.

Moran said he had often picked up small parcels for Batter at Zetter's Radio and TV Shop. He had also delivered several stuffed animals from Batter to a certain address in Bayport. Two men there had recently paid him to spy on the Hardys.

"What kind of racket were they up to?" barked a detective.

Moran cringed fearfully. "I told you I don't know! Batter warned me not to get snoopy!"

"The picture's clear enough," Fenton Hardy said.

"Zetter made the electronic bugs, and Batter implanted them in the stuffed animals."

"And it explains why that baldheaded crook picked Zetter's shop to duck through when he was running away with the wolf's head!" said Joe.

"We already have an alarm out for Zetter," put in chief Collis, "but he's not at his shop or his house."

Frank, meanwhile, was scanning a wall map of the Bayport area, locating the address Moran had named. "Look! It's directly in the path of the scrambler beam!" he exclaimed.

"There's a squad car standing by," said Collig. "We were just waiting for you."

The Hardys' convertible followed close behind as the police car raced through the streets of Bayport. In minutes they were screeching to a halt outside a shabby-looking frame house in a run-down, older part of town. All the windows were dark, and high hedges separated the house from its neighbours.

"Ten to one the place is empty," said Mr Hardy as he and the boys leapt from the convertible. "The gang probably pulled out right after the bug was discovered."

The investigator's guess proved correct. Two camp cots, a rickety table, and chairs had been left behind, as well as a litter of empty food cans, but there were clear signs of a hasty exit. Lengths of ripped-out wiring and scattered, broken electronic components in an upstairs room showed where there radio gear had been set up.

"This was their listening post, all right," said the FBI agent.

"Get the fingerprint boys busy!" Collig snapped to a detective-sergeant.

The room, evidently the master bedroom, had a fireplace in one corner. Joe noticed a small heap of ashes on the hearth, as if papers had been burned hastily. One scrap, although charred beyond recognition, was still intact.

"Hey, Dad!" Joe exclaimed. "Think we might get anything from this?"

Fenton Hardy squatted down to examine the paper remnant. "It's worth a try."

Chief Collig willingly agreed to leave the task in the Hardys skilled hands. The charred paper was gently swept on to a glass plate, then sprayed with a fixative, and flattened under another plate. Later, in the boys' crime lab at home, the scrap was photographed on an orthochromatic plate and printed on high-contrast paper.

Three words could now be made out in a ghostly scrawl:

Aardvark to Canada

19

A Wrecked Canoe

"I'll bet this was part of a code message!" Joe exclaimed, staring at the photograph of the burnt paper.

"And 'Aardvark' may be Nils Afron," said Frank.

"Yes, it's not hard to guess what happened," their father said thoughtfully. "The gang members in Bayport no doubt radioed Afron as soon as the bug was discovered. Then he sent back this code message saying to clear out and that he himself was going to Canada."

"Canada!" Joe echoed excitedly. "If he wants to lie low, he might go back to that hunting lodge in Ontario!"

Mr Hardy nodded. "It's a good possibility. Let's find out exactly where the lodge is located."

All three hurried to Fenton Hardy's study. Checking an atlas, they discovered that Lake Okemow lay in the James Bay area and that the nearest town appeared to be Moosonee.

Mr Hardy glanced at his watch. "Almost ten-thirty. Hmm. I suppose it's possible we might learn something by calling there, even at this hour."

Frank and Joe stood by tensely as their father picked up the telephone on his desk and dialled long-distance. He asked to be put through directly to the operator in Moosonee, Ontario.

When the connection was made, the detective asked, "Can you tell me any way to contact the Lachine Hunting Lodge on Lake Okemow?"

"There is no phone service, sir. The only way to reach the lodge directly is by radio."

"Radio?" Mr Hardy shot a glance at the boys. "You mean over the ham bands?"

"Yes, sir." In answer to the detective's question, she gave the lodge owner's call letters and the usual frequency for local-area hams. "Mr Lachine's on the air every night about this time, if you want to try contacting him."

"Thank you. We shall," Fenton Hardy replied.

The Hardys went to the attic radio shack and warmed up their rig. Frank tuned in a number of conversations on the 40-metre band until he caught Lachine's call sign. Then he zeroed in on the lodge owner's frequency and waited for his transmission to end.

"I have not much hope for him, *mon ami*," Lachine was saying, "but keep your eyes open when you are tending your trap line. The bush pilots will all be looking, of course."

"Sounds as if someone's lost," Joe muttered.

As soon as they heard Lachine ending his conversation with the local ham, Frank called and quickly made contact. He introduced himself and asked about Nils Afron.

"Afron? *Bon tonnerre!*" The lodge owner sounded deeply shaken. "What a sad coincidence that tonight you should call to inquire for him. I am much afraid that M'sieu Afron may be dead."

"Dead!" Frank gasped. "What happened to him? You mean some sort of accident?"

"*Oui*, it appears he has drowned." Lachine explained that Afron had flown in that very day from Timmins, Ontario, arriving just before one o'clock. After a brief lunch, he had started up river on a fishing trip, without a guide.

"I did not like him going alone," Lachine added, "but he is an old and valued guest. When he insists, what can I say? He had trouble on his mind, I believe, and wished to be away from everyone. Then tonight an Indian comes running to the lodge and tells us he has sighted M'sieu Afron's wrecked canoe. It was washed ashore up river from here. *Sacrebleu!* A terrible tragedy!"

"You think there's no hope for him?" Frank asked. "Maybe he went ashore and the canoe drifted loose."

"Perhaps. Time alone will tell, but I fear the worst," Lachine said sadly.

After talking a while longer, Frank signed off and turned to Joe and Mr Hardy. "Well, what do you think?"

"Sounds fishy to me!" Joe declared.

"Could be a trick, all right," Mr Hardy agreed. "Just a clever way for Afron to make the police think he's dead." The investigator scowled and rubbed his jaw. "Well, from here on it's a job for the Canadian Mounties, I guess."

Frank and Joe glanced at each other, both struck with the same impulse.

"Dad," Frank spoke up, "why couldn't Joe and I go up there and look around? You still have plenty to do running down the rest of the gang. In the meantime, we might be able to pick up a clue that would prove whether Afron's really dead."

Joe chimed in. "That's a swell idea, Dad! What do you say? We'd only miss two days of school and get back right after the weekend!"

Mr Hardy was thoughtful a moment, then smiled. "All right. Why not? You two have certainly earned a trip, with your work on this case!"

Chet Morton stopped at the house early the next morning on his way to school. He had heard on the breakfast newscast about the raid on the gang's listening post and was avid for a firsthand account from the Hardys. Frank and Joe gave him the details, then told about their projected trip to Canada.

"We'll be catching the two o'clock flight," Frank ended.

"You lucky lads!" The stout boy added darkly, "All the same, I wouldn't want to be in *your* shoes. What if you run into Afron out in the woods somewhere?"

"Don't worry, we plan to stalk him in our moose disguise," Joe said with a wink at his brother. "Remember, the Hardys always get their man!"

Much of the morning was spent in frantic packing, amid worried advice from Aunt Gertrude. Each of the Hardy boys loaded a good-sized duffel bag with his bedroll, heavy woollen clothing, boots, socks, and other needed items. Frank crammed their father's small, portable battery transceiver into his bag, while Joe stowed away a compact, inflatable rubber life raft.

Shortly after one o'clock they were surprised by a visit from Jimmy Gordon and his mother. "I saw Chet on the way to school this morning and he told me where you're going," Jimmy explained. "When I told Ma at lunchtime, we decided to come over and say goodbye."

"I – Well, I just thought I should apologize for being so short with you boys the other day," Mrs Gordon said hesitantly.

"That's all right," Frank said. "We understand."

"I wanted to thank you, too, for being so kind to Jimmy. His teacher says he's perked up wonderfully in school." Mrs Gordon's eyes moistened and she gave Jimmy a hug. "I'm changing to a different job next week, so I'll be able to spend more time with him."

Jimmy pulled out a package and handed it to Frank and Joe. "Here's a present to take with you. I paid for 'em with my own dough!"

The parcel contained two small jackknives. They were flimsy in quality and not likely to be useful for much more than sharpening pencils, but the Hardys assured Jimmy they were exactly what was needed for the trip.

"You really like 'em?" The boys's face beamed. "I'm sure glad! I figured hunting knives would come in handy up there in the woods."

Soon after the Gordons left, Frank and Joe gave Aunt Gertrude a final hug and set off for the airport with their father. Their route included Toronto, then over a vast, lonely, region, splashed with lakes and carpeted with spruce.

The plane landed briefly at Sudbury, where the boys glimpsed the white domes of a radar station standing out against the night sky. Two hours after leaving Toronto, they set down near the rugged mining town of Timmins.

They registered at a hotel for the night and arranged by telephone for a bush pilot to fly them on to Lake Okemow. At daybreak the two sleuths were up and breakfasting on a hearty meal of Canadian bacon, eggs, and fried potatoes. Then they taxied off in a four-seater amphibian.

The flight proved to be bumpy. Below lay a dense wilderness of black spruce, poplar, birch, and tamarack. Glittering lakes and snakelike streams slashed the forest. Farther north came barren patches, frosted white with snow. Then again they were flying over heavy timber.

"Here we are!" the pilot said at last. He brought the plane down to a choppy landing on the not-yet-frozen lake and taxied to a wooden pier. On the shore lay the stout log hunting lodge. Smoke feathered from its chimney.

A biting wind clawed at their faces as a bearded red-haired man in a plaid Mackinaw came cruncing across the snow to meet them.

"*Bonjour!*" he boomed. "I was not expecting guests, but welcome to my lodge!"

"We're the Hardy boys," Frank said as they shook hands. "I'm Frank and this is my brother Joe. I talked to you on the radio. Remember?"

"Ah, *mais oui!* And I am Jacques Lachine!" He

bellowed an order, and a big, dark-skinned man came out to get the boys' duffel bags.

As Lachine led the way to the lodge, he remarked that guests were usually few at this time of year but that business suddenly appeared to have picked up. "First, M'sieu Afron comes on Wednesday. Now you two, and today I hear by radio another gentleman will arrive tomorrow from New York, a M'sieu Ardmore."

The boys looked at each other but said nothing until they were alone in their room at the lodge. Then Joe said, "Did you get that name Ardmore?"

Frank nodded thoughtfully. "I sure did. Sort of close to 'Aardvark', isn't it?" Both wondered if they had made a mistake about Afron being the leader of the gang.

As they ate lunch in front of a roaring fire, Lachine reported that there was still no news of Afron. Frank explained that they had come expressly to help search for him and would like to make a trip upriver to look for clues.

Lachine shook his head doubtfully. "The weather looks bad, *mes amis*, but if you insist upon going, my man René will be your guide."

Within a hour after the meal, the boys had loaded their duffel bags into a canoe and were pushing off, up the mouth of the nearby river, into the wilderness. René, the dark-skinned man, rowed astern while Frank and Joe took turns wielding the bow paddle.

On both sides of them lay a dense forest of towering evergreens. Ice was forming along the banks, which in places were strewn with rugged boulders or rose in steep, rocky upthrusts.

As the afternoon wore on, the wind grew stronger and more bitter. Dark clouds closed in from the northwest. René muttered, "The snow, she come soon, I think."

The first flakes came in gusts but gradually the storm increased to a howling blizzard. Soon after dark the trio reached the clearing where Afron had planned to camp.

René beached the canoe against the hilly bank. He ordered the boys to go ahead while he unloaded the camping gear. Shouldering their duffel bags, Frank and Joe clambered up the slope.

There were signs that the spot had been used as a frequent campsite by hunting and fishing parties. The two boys selected a sheltered spot close to the trees and began looking for firewood. Minutes went by.

"Wonder what's keeping René," Joe said.

In the snowy darkness it was difficult to see more than a few yards. Puzzled by the guide's delay, the Hardy's made their way back towards the shore to see if he was having trouble.

Frank was the first to reach the riverbank. His eyes widened in dismay as he peered all around. "Joe!" he gasped. "The canoe's gone!"

20

The Right Spots

The boys were thunderstruck to find themselves alone on the night-shrouded, icy shore.

"You don't suppose René got swept down river somehow while he was unloading?" Joe faltered.

"Not a chance! He had the canoe too well beached," Frank said.

The Hardys shouted the guide's name frantically, but knew their voices could not carry far in the shrieking blizzard. Bit by bit the realization grew that they had been deserted!

"Either René's in cahoots with Afron," Frank said bitterly, "or he and Lachine both are."

Joe nodded. "Now we know why Afron used the lodge for drumming up spy-ring victims."

"Also why he came here to hide from the law!"

The boys debated whether to try trekking back downriver. For long stretches the banks were impossible to negotiate on foot, yet once out of sight of the stream they might quickly become lost! Without food or matches, their plight seemed desperte.

"Wait a second!" Joe exclaimed. "We're forgetting about Dad's transceiver! Maybe we can call some ham in this area for help!"

Frank hesitated, then shook his head. "Too risky.

Don't forget, Lachine's on the air every night. If he heard our call, he and René might come back and hunt us down."

Joe paced back and forth, swinging his arms to keep warm. "What about the life raft? Think we could make it downriver on that?"

Frank weighed the odds. "The river's freezing fast. If we hit any ice, we'd be goners."

On the other hand, the boys thought any move seemed preferable to staying where they were. If they returned to Lake Okemow, they might be able to filch supplies from the lodge until some form of help arrived from the outside.

"Okay. Let's try it!" Frank said.

Joe inflated the raft with a CO_2 cartridge while Frank cut tree boughs to use as sweeps. Taking only blankets, a flashlight, and the transceiver, they pushed off downriver.

Almost at once the raft was seized in the fast current. The Hardys worked frantically, fending off jagged ice and trying to control their frail bark. The wind stung their faces as they steered into the swirling blizzard. At times the curving river put the wind cross-stream, threatening to beach or capsize the raft.

The snow-filled darkness increased their danger, making it hard to see obstructions or changes in course. Numb with cold, Frank and Joe continued on doggedly.

Hours went by, and the boys had lost all track of time, when at last the wilderness seemed to open and they found themselves approaching the river mouth.

Poling their craft ashore, the Hardys flopped exhausted on the riverbank.

Not far away lay the lodge, its windows aglow with light. After hiding their raft, the boys crept up to the building and peered inside.

Lachine, René, and three other men were seated comfortably around the fireplace. They were talking and laughing as they drank mugs of steaming coffee. Frank and Joe identified Lachine's 'guests' almost at once. The biggest one, blond and pug-nosed, was undoubtedly Afron. The other two were the auction thieves!

"Those dirty rats!" Joe mumbled. "And they think we're freezing to death out in the woods!"

The lodge's radio gear was in plain view.

"Keep watch and tell me if Lachine goes on the air!" Frank hissed. He squatted down in the snow and hoisted the transceiver antenna.

Within minutes he succeeded in contacting a ham at Moose Factory. He hastily explained the situation. The ham, who was outraged to hear of Lachine's treachery, soon reported back that a plane would take off from the island post as soon as the weather abated.

"Looks as if this blizzard could keep up till morning," Joe muttered.

"We'll be lucky if it stops then," Frank said.

A lean-to storage shed adjoined the lodge. To evade the bone-chilling wind, the boys decided to take shelter inside until daybreak. Wrapped in their blankets, they settled down against a pile of logs. Soon both were nodding.

Frank awoke with a start hours later. Daylight was

showing through chinks in the shed. Steps came crunching closer in the snow outside.

Frank jerked wide awake. He shook his brother. A hand fumbled at the latch outside, then the door creaked open. The dark face of René, the guide, gaped in astonishment at the two boys.

Frank sprang at the man before he could cry out. Joe seized his leg and the burly guide flopped backward into the snow. But there was no chance to clap a hand over his mouth. René bellowed like a wounded ox.

The man was tremendously powerful. He shook off the two youths easily. One swipe of his huge fist sent Frank spinning into a snowbank. By this time, Lachine and the two auction thieves were running from the lodge. René stunned Joe with a blow, then grabbed him in a crushing bear hug. The others overpowered Frank.

"So, *mes enfants!*" Lachine leered at the two boys. "You prefer us to deal with you here, instead of dying in the wilderness, eh?"

The men were dragging Frank and Joe towards the lodge entrance when Nils Afron came striding out. He grinned in vicious satisfaction.

"So the brats got back alive. Now we'll make 'em pay for causing us so much trouble!"

"You're the ones in trouble!" Joe flared back. "Soapy Moran's in jail and Zetter soon will be. We know all about your racket!"

Afron sneered. "That won't help you boys."

The baldheaded thug muttered angrily, "I knew it was a mistake hiring Moran to spy on them. That cheap con artist had to put us all in danger for a measly ten-buck swindle!"

"It wasn't Moran who blew the whistle on us," his fat partner said. "We'd still be tuning in on Lektrex if these kids hadn't traced the bug!"

"Forget it!" Afron snapped. "Our Philly crew and the West Coast crew haven't been nabbed yet. We'll all be back in business before long."

At the droning sound of an approaching plane, Afron and his henchmen turned their heads skyward. An amphibian was swooping down towards the lake! Lachine gasped.

"Sacrebleu! M'sieu Ardmore arrive, I think!"

Frank and Joe took advantage of the distraction. They jerked free from their captors and dashed into the woods. Afron and his men pursued them as the Hardys dodged through the trees, towards the lake.

Meanwhile, the plane landed and taxied to the pier. A tall, broad-shouldered man leapt out, followed by two Mounties in parkas.

Glancing back, Frank saw Lachine's face go ashen with fear. His panic-stricken pals scattered, but the loud crack of revolver shots brought them to a frightened halt.

In minutes Afron, Lachine, René, and the two gangsters were lined up in front of the lodge, their hands raised in surrender.

"Dad!" Joe gasped as the tall man embraced his two sons. "Don't tell me you were Ardmore?"

The grinning detective nodded. "I thought you two might need some help in smoking out Afron, but it seems you've already done it alone."

Mr Hardy explained that the blizzard had threatened to delay his arrival. Nevertheless, he had contacted the Mounties on landing at Timmins. After hearing of his sons' call for help, he had managed to find a bush pilot willing to fly him to Moose Factory.

All five prisoners were taken to the Mountie post. Lachine and René were charged with plotting the Hardy boys' deaths. Afron and his two men were held for extradition to the United States.

Not until Sunday afternoon were the Hardys able to take off from Moose Factory. A Mounted Police officer told them Afron had seized a jailer's gun and tried to escape, but had been unsuccessful.

"Dangerous as a snake, that fellow," the Mountie commented. "He boasted he'd been in too many tight spots to be taken by any backwoods cops. But this is one spot he won't leave without wearing handcuffs."

Frank was thoughtful on the flight to Timmins.

"What's on your mind?" Joe asked, curious.

"I'm just thinking about what the Mountie told us, and what Jimmy's uncle told *him*."

Joe stared at his brother. Suddenly his eyes lit up. "Wow! If you're right, Frank, Batter's treasure was right under our noses!"

Mr Hardy listened keenly as the boys explained. "It's a clever hunch," he agreed.

Early Monday afternoon they arrived in Bayport. Frank made two quick telephone calls.

"Mrs Batter sold the house Saturday," he reported. "She's there now, clearing out the last few items so the new owner can move in."

"What about Jimmy?" Joe asked.

"We can pick him up at school."

Joe chuckled. "Let's get Chet, too. He has a right to see the end of this."

Later, as the three Hardys, Jimmy, and Chet drove up to the former Batter estate, they saw Mrs Batter near the garage. She was adding several items to a pile of trash and furniture.

"Well!" she said coldly. "I hear you caught those thieves."

"Yes," said Frank. "I'm sorry we never did get back your animals."

Mrs Batter sniffed. "No matter. I may as well tell you, my husband hinted he'd hidden something valuable in the house – but I'm sure now it was just talk. That was Elias all over!"

"Mind if we look through this trash?"

"Go ahead. You won't find anything."

Joe was already exricating "D. Carson's" stuffed, speckled king snake from the pile.

Seeing its speckles, Jimmy blurted excitedly. "So that's what Uncle Elly meant by looking 'in the right spots'."

"Maybe," Frank said. He fingered the body of the snake tensely. Then, using a length of wire he had brought, the young detective fished down through the snake's gaping mouth.

There were gasps as Frank pulled back the wire. Dangling from its hooked end was a necklace of glittering pear-shaped diamonds!

"The Crescent necklace!" Joe said. "Pretty tricky of Batter to use fake nameplates to throw everyone off the scent!"

"Give me that!" Mrs Batter cried.

"No, you don't!" Jimmy snapped. "This belongs to a store and it's going back there!"

"Good for you, son," said Fenton hardy. "I wonder what's on that paper."

A paper strip was tightly rolled around part of the necklace. Frank removed and opened it.

"It's some sort of typed confession!"

The closely spaced typing gave a complete account of the Aardvark gang's industrial espionage activities, including names, descriptions, and hideouts of all members. Batter's statement told of his own work on the bugged animals and said he was putting the information about his pals down on paper as an "insurance policy" to keep the gang from double-crossing him or harming him.

At Bayport Police Headquarters, Fenton Hardy made a long call to Toronto, where Afron and his two cohorts had been taken to await extradition to the United States. When he hung up, the investigator smiled with grim satisfaction.

"Baldy has just talked. Seems he's still sore over the way his partner left him stranded at the Lektrex plant. He's willing to waive extradition and testify as a government witness."

The gangster, Mr Hardy reported, said that Batter had demanded more and more money from the gang for his work. When Afron balked at paying it and threatened him, Batter had warned that a written confession about the gang was hidden in a safe place in Bayport and would be turned over to the police if anything happened to him.

"Something Batter said convinced Afron the confession was hidden in one of the stuffed animals," Mr Hardy went on. "That's why they tried so hard to round up all samples of Batter's work in Bayport. Finally they even took the stuffed fox from Lektrex and looked in *it*." The animals had later been dumped in the bay.

Afron had alerted his men in Bayport when Mr Hardy returned from Europe. The two thugs had trailed the Hardys' car from the airport to the restaurant, hoping to steal and examine his case report. But Baldy had had time only to snatch back their antenna before being seen.

"Well, we nabbed Zetter yesterday," said Collig, "so I'd say the case is about closed."

The police chief turned to Jimmy. "It's a good thing your uncle found the necklace too hot to dispose of, young fellow. There's a five-thousand-dollar reward still standing for its recovery."

"Five *thousand?*" Jimmy whistled in awe and looked at the Hardys. "Will I get part of it?"

Frank and Joe grinned, though they were sorry their sleuthing activities were over for the time being. Very soon, however, they were to start solving the case of *The Secret Panel*.

"Jimmy, the money is yours," said Frank. "You gave us the first clue."

"Oh, boy!" Jimmy yelled excitedly. "Wait'll Ma hears this! And say, she was going to bake a big chocolate cake for you guys. I hope it's the kind you like!"

"Are you kidding?" Chet licked his lips. "Let's go sample it right now and I'll give you an expert opinion!"

The Hardy Boys Mystery Stories

ARMADA

All these books are available at your local bookshop or newsagent, or can be ordered from the publisher. To order direct from the publishers just tick the title you want and fill in the form below:

Name _____

Address _____

_____

Send to: Collins Childrens Cash Sales
PO Box 11
Falmouth
Cornwall
TR10 9EN

Please enclose a cheque or postal order or debit my Visa/ Access –

Credit card no:

Expiry date:

Signature:

– to the value of the cover price plus:

UK: 60p for the first book, 25p for the second book, plus 15p per copy for each additional book ordered to a maximum charge of £1.90.

BFPO: 60p for the first book, 25p for the second book plus 15p per copy for the next 7 books, thereafter 9p per book.

Overseas and Eire: £1.25 for the first book, 75p for the second book. Thereafter 28p per book.

Armada reserve the right to show new retail prices on covers which may differ from those previously advertised in the text or elswhere.

ARMADA